The Necromancer's Apprentice
Copyright © 2014 Icy Sedgwick
ISBN 978 1 9807 2217 5

Cover Illustration by Daniël Hugo.
Cover Design by Icy Sedgwick.

Third Edition © 2018

This second paperback edition was printed by KDP Print.

An e-book edition of this title is also available.

www.icysedgwick.com

THE
NECROMANCER'S
APPRENTICE

Book 1 in the Underground City Series

by Icy Sedgwick

Other books by Icy Sedgwick

The Grey o' Donnell Series
The Guns of Retribution
To Kill A Dead Man

Short Story Collections
Checkmate: Tales of Speculative Fiction
Harbingers: Dark Tales of Speculative
Fiction

The Underground City Series
The Necromancer's Apprentice
The Necromancer's Rogue

BEFORE WE GET STARTED...

If you enjoy this book, please take the time to leave a short review at whatever retailer's site you purchased it from. Reviews help other readers find good books!

You can also get an exclusive prequel story from my website – but more on that at the end of the book.

Buckle in, keep your arms inside the car at all times, and enjoy the ride!

For Anubis and Bast.

CHAPTER 1

Jyx put down his quill and stared at the open texts before him. Professor Tourney required four incantations to be written from scratch, and he needed to practice his sigil-writing for Madam Edifer. He looked at the books and sighed. The problem with homework was not the "work" part of the equation. No, Jyx usually completed the set tasks in half the time of his classmates. Rather, it was the "home" part with which he had difficulty.

His cramped garret room was not an ideal location for study. His narrow window overlooked the clamour and stench of Benefactor's Close, and the accumulated dirt clinging to the panes prevented all but the most persistent light from entering his room. Rats scuttled behind the walls, and the dying embers in the grate no longer gave out any measurable heat. His study candle, the very candle his mother had scrimped and saved for six months to buy, was now less than an inch tall, and splattered more hot wax across the desk than light across his work.

Jyx shoved back the chair, wincing as the feet scraped across the decayed floorboards. The shouts of his five siblings drifted up the narrow staircase to the garret, followed by his mother's plaintive pleas for quiet. He marvelled at their ability to make more noise than the traders in the close outside. Their nonsensical games and absurd habits often made him consider the fact he may well be a changeling, accidentally deposited with his mother instead of a well-groomed gentlewoman in the City Above.

On cue, Jyx took up the hand-painted post-card from his desk. It depicted a wide, tree-lined boulevard. White brick villas and manicured lawns faced each other across the street. Jyx dreamed of a life in the City Above, a life of natural light and clean air. Missa, the only student in his class who didn't despise him, had slipped him the postcard during a class on banishing. One day, once he'd passed his exams and become a fully licensed mage, he too would live there and enjoy fresh water and open space.

"Jyximus!" His mother's voice screeched through the garret's foetid atmosphere. Jyx sighed, replaced the postcard on his desk, and trudged downstairs.

The grime of the Underground City streaked the windows of the lower rooms. Flickers of gas-light from the lamp outside penetrated the gloom.

His mother sat in a rotting chair by the cold fireplace, a pile of mending in a broken basket on the floor. She hunched over someone's shirt, repairing a tear. Jyx couldn't tell whose shirt it was.

"I've sent your brothers and sisters down to the market, but gods know there won't be much left at this time," she said.

"At least whatever they do have will be cheap." Jyx glanced at the clock above the fireplace. Five o'clock in the evening. He frowned. There was no such thing as time in the Underground City, only varying degrees of darkness.

"Jyx, stop daydreaming. Make yourself useful and sort that lot out on the table." His mother gestured to a pile of whitish dust on an old plate. Jyx pulled up a stool and turned himself so he wouldn't cast his own shadow across the work to be done.

To stretch their food budget, his mother liked to preserve whatever meat she could get her hands on. She bought the cheapest salt available from a less-than-reputable trader in Mercer's Close. Jyx despised the trader, but he despised his tendency to mix the salt with sand even more. Jyx's evening task was to separate the grains, giving his mother valuable salt, and himself sand to use in his experiments.

"How much sand do you need?" she asked.

"Just a handful this time. I managed to enchant the last batch."

"Oh!" She looked up from her work, pride etched into her worn features. "What did it do?"

"I used it to plug a hole in my shoe." Jyx slipped off the leather boot and showed his mother the hole near the toe on the outside of the sole then pointed to the smooth, sand-coloured patch on the inside of the shoe. Only a keen eye, or a magickal background, would recognise the patch as an enchantment.

"Why, that's a helpful little thing to have learnt!"

"I know. I thought you'd like that one."

His mother beamed at him with pride. Jyx smiled; maybe her sacrifices to get him a place at the Academy wouldn't be for nothing.

Jyx returned to his work. He drew a sigil with his finger on the woodwork of the table, and poured a handful of the salty sand over it. The sand clung to the mark, but the salt bounced up and down, unable to settle. Jyx swept his hand under the bouncing salt, catching the grains in his palm. This spell wasn't exactly on the syllabus at the Academy, but it was amazing what you could find in the library if you had the nerve to go looking for it.

Half an hour passed before the salt and sand lay on separate plates. The door burst open as Jyx erased the sigil. His brothers and sisters piled into the room, parading their purchases in front of their mother. She inspected bread so hard she could use it to knock in nails, and passed judgement on the scraps of flesh more fat than meat. Mould bloomed on the crust of the wheel of cheese, and the fruit looked mere hours away from complete decay.

"Very good, children. Run and wash your hands while I make us some supper," Jyx's mother said. The youngsters thundered out of the room. Jyx stood and headed to the door.

"Won't you have some supper, Jyx?"

"I find I'm not hungry tonight, Mother. I'll see you in the morning."

Jyx's stomach rumbled but he just couldn't face a mouldy supper again. Besides, he could eat tomorrow at the Academy. It was better that his brothers and sisters were fed. He cast a forlorn look at the near inedible food and headed for the stairs. It was not the first time he would go to bed hungry, and more than likely it would not be the last.

* * * *

A cock crowed in the depths of the Underground City. Prodded into life by one of the Time Keepers, it announced the dawn that none of the inhabitants could see. Jyx groaned and threw back his threadbare blanket. He swung his legs out of the narrow cot and picked his way across the floor, mindful to avoid the sleeping forms of his siblings. He snatched up his satchel from where it lay beside his desk.

An iron basin and a chipped jug of water sat on the dining table. Jyx washed his face and hands in the tepid water, and left the washing things for his brothers and sisters. There wouldn't be any more fresh water until lunchtime, by which point Jyx would be long gone.

"Ah, you're up. Would you like some breakfast?" His mother bustled out of the poky pantry beside the small kitchen range.

"No, I haven't got time. What are you doing up so early?" Jyx shrugged into the robes hung up to dry before the fire. He allowed himself to enjoy the brief flurry of warmth as they settled against his skin.

"It's washing day, Jyx. I have a lot to get through."

Jyx frowned, thinking of his mother's work-load, and swung his satchel onto his shoulder. His mother held out a puckered apple, and he slipped it into his bag. He could always eat it during morning break if he hid behind the well—the other boys would never let him hear the end of it if they caught him eating such rotten fruit.

"Now you have yourself a good day, Jyx. Learn all you can and remember to respect your elders."

Jyx rolled his eyes and kissed his mother on the cheek before descending the three flights of stairs to the street. The narrow close was already full of hawkers and peddlers, and a night lady winked at him as she sashayed past in mismatched heeled boots. He watched her round bottom sway from side to side for a few moments before snapping out of his trance. Night ladies could end up being very expensive if they caught you in their thrall—or so he'd been told. Some of the wealthier boys would "slum it" in the Underground City, looking for thrills, and they told tall tales of what they got up to.

Jyx threaded his way upwards through the

maze of alleys and closes. A meandering path took him out of the centre of the Underground City, and he trudged up the worn steps towards Lockervar's Gate. Eight feet wide and fifteen feet tall, the gate kept the inhabitants of the Underground City from pestering those in the City Above. That was the theory, although everyone knew there was more than one way out.

"'Alt, who is it?"

A guard stepped out of a lopsided wooden hut beside the massive gate. He wore the typical battered leather armour of the Underground City Guard, and his helmet seemed three sizes too big for him. He clutched a bent halberd in his shaking hands, and Jyx wondered why the Guard would recruit someone scarcely older than himself.

"I'm a student at the Academy," Jyx replied.

"'Course you are, 'n I'm a wood elf." The guard attempted a sneer but he looked more like he was trying to suppress a sneeze.

Jyx sighed and rummaged in his satchel for his Academy identification. He held out the small square of burgundy leather, bearing his name in gold letters, and an embossed sigil.

"What do I do with that, then?"

Another guard appeared from behind the hut, tucking his leggings behind his leather codpiece. Jyx didn't need to guess what he'd been doing— the smell of ammonia was overpowering.

"What's the trouble?" asked the guard.

"Your assistant won't accept my identification." Jyx showed the leather square to the newcomer.

"All right, do yer thing then."

Jyx uttered a single word and the sigil lit up, its glow the same shade of gold as the lettering. The newcomer nodded and waved Jyx through. Only the bearer of the square could accomplish that feat. The younger guard pouted and stomped back into the hut as Jyx walked past.

The stone city lay beneath a pale blue sky, still tinted with the purple and pink of the dawn. Craftsmen and traders busied themselves with the setup of their stalls along the thoroughfare that led from the gate into the Artists' Quarter. Jyx looked at their plump fruit and fresh bread with hungry eyes, but an empty purse hung from his belt. The traders gave him suspicious glances and a wide berth as he walked past.

A busy network of canals crisscrossed the Artists' Quarter, and Jyx spotted several painters or poets hanging out of upper windows, staring into the green water below. Jyx had never studied art or literature, except where it was relevant to his magickal studies, but he didn't think they'd find their muse in the canals.

People queued at the nearest jetty. A massive man with slick black hair and a perfectly sculpted handlebar moustache waved them this way and that, dispensing them into the gondolas and ferries that traversed the canals of the quarter. He spotted Jyx and nodded, pointing towards a rotten jetty farther along the street. A tall man, as thin as the other was broad, leaned against the wall. A cigarillo hung from his narrow lips and a floppy hat shaded his eyes from the early morning sun.

"Ah, Master Faire."

"Just going to the Academy, Pickford. Same as usual."

Jyx hopped down into the battered gondola, and set his satchel between his feet. Pickford stepped down behind him, bringing with him a waft of cigarillo smoke and stale meat sandwiches.

"You're sure I can't interest you in something else?"

"No, Pickford. Academy, ho!"

Jyx pointed along the canal and laughed. Pickford giggled, a peculiar nasal sound, and pushed away from the jetty. The gondolier tried to divert Jyx towards less wholesome activities than school daily, and it had become something of a standing joke between the pair. Jyx missed him on those days when he ran the more mundane routes, and Jyx was ferried by Knoxxos, the giant with the ginger goatee.

The gondola slid through the water, the sounds of the Artists' Quarter fading as they drew away from the main canals. A single canal cut through this side of the quarter, and the neighbouring Warlock Hill, on the way to the Academy. Nearly all of the other students lived in the City Above, and travelled to school by coach or foot. Only Jyx, from his lowly home in the Underground City, arrived by canal.

"So how is the schooling, my young friend?" Pickford asked.

"Same as usual. The teachers go through the basic stuff for everyone else, and I get bored because I learned it last year. But I have to pretend like I'm interested."

"It's the same for anybody who's good at something. They will catch you up and you will all learn together, I am sure."

Jyx frowned at the water. He didn't want his classmates to catch up to him. As bored as he often got, he liked being ahead of them. It was the only thing that almost made it worthwhile to be a total outcast.

The pastel-coloured buildings gave way to the austere white residences of Warlock Hill. Flashes of coloured light escaped through cracks in the tight shutters, and Jyx wondered what sorcery went on within the workshops and laboratories that overlooked the canals. Pickford pointed out a night lady, sunning herself at an open window, and Jyx gasped.

"You are not the only one from below up here, no?" Pickford smirked.

Eventually the canal left Warlock Hill behind, and meandered through the grounds of the Academy. Jyx caught flashes of it through the trees, its gleaming towers and elegant spires reflecting the morning sun. On several occasions, Jyx spotted a raven. Every time he noticed the bird perched on a wall or a pillar, it paused to preen its feathers until the gondola passed. Jyx preferred to think that a bird keeper had lost his menagerie. After all, why would a raven follow him to school?

Pickford guided the gondola towards a dilapidated jetty and helped Jyx scramble out of the boat. Jyx thanked him and hurried along the jet-ty towards the gravelled walk that led to the main building. He clutched Pickford's wooden token in his pocket; if he didn't hand it to Administrator Wexen, Pickford wouldn't be paid.

Jyx walked along the path that led around the side of the main building and came out on the main walk that ran all the way to the entrance gates. A low hubbub filled the air as students alighted from coaches or sent accompanying servants on their way. Jyx slipped into the throng making their way up the wide staircase towards the entrance doors, and headed inside for another day of tedious lectures. Still, he'd rather be listening to a lecture about a charm he already knew than be scrubbing floors in the Underground City. Besides, there was always another library visit to excite him.

CHAPTER 2

Jyx sat at the back of the class and held open his incantations textbook, hoping that Professor Tourney wouldn't notice the slim volume of *Pithman's Advanced Geomagicae* resting inside. At the front of the class, Reetha Edstow recited her incantations in a dull monotone. Jyx snorted. He didn't know what outcome Reetha had intended, but if she'd been trying to bore the entire class to death, then she was doing something right. Missa sat near the front of the class. Judging by the tilt of her head, she'd fallen asleep.

The earth magick book demanded his wandering attention once more. He found the language a little dry, but his experiments always worked. He smiled when he flicked past the sigil to separate salt and sand. Later this afternoon, he would start the chapter on earth divination.

Perhaps he could make a little extra money for his mother down at the market. Living in the Underground City bred desperation, and its inhabitants were always looking for some form of comfort, even from fortune-tellers.

"Pssst."

Markus Prady wanted his attention. Markus always wanted his attention. Jyx didn't necessarily want to dislike Markus, as he was one of the few students who didn't trip him up, manifest mud in his satchel or try to turn his hair green, but Markus lacked many of the social skills that might otherwise make him a good friend.

"Jyx. Hey, Jyx."

Jyx put a finger to his lips and glanced sideways at Markus. The last thing he needed was Professor Tourney coming to the back of the class to ask why they weren't paying attention. Advanced earth magick wasn't exactly on the syllabus for the term.

"Pssst."

Markus wiggled his fingers at him. Jyx scrawled *Prof T will hear* across a scrap scroll and underlined the phrase twice. Markus's stupid gaze travelled from Jyx's spiky handwriting to Professor Tourney and finally to Jyx himself. A spark of understanding flickered and died in Markus's eyes.

The shrivelled mage glanced in Jyx's direction. Jyx sat staring dead ahead, pasting a look of total immersion on his face. The professor looked away again. Jyx let out the breath he hadn't realised he'd been holding.

"Jyx. Pssst. What's that?"

The tip of Markus's feather quill tickled the edge of Jyx's vision. He snorted, knowing to turn any further would bring the professor back there, asking why he wasn't listening to Reetha.

"It's none of your concern," Jyx hissed through his teeth.

"That's advanced stuff."

Jyx turned and glared at Markus. The older boy fell silent and turned away, apparently keen to avoid the heat of Jyx's gaze.

The book bore the brunt of his glare instead. Jyx flicked to the final chapter, labelled Homunculi. Jyx broke into a grin, swiftly hidden behind the book to avoid detection, as he came across an illustration of men made of clay. In the drawing, some held tools while others followed their human masters, loaded with heavy burdens. There was definitely a market for homunculi in the Underground City, and if he could figure out how to make one...

He turned the page and stifled an exclamation of annoyance. Two jagged strips of paper nestled in the crease between the last page and the next. The list of ingredients was present on the back of the illustrated page, but the pages containing the necessary sigils and incantations were missing. Jyx cursed under his breath. If he had his way, it would become a capital offence to deface a library book.

Muted applause broke at that moment and Jyx looked up. Reetha returned to her seat, her face red. Professor Tourney peered after her, his papery face as impassive as ever. Jyx always thought the old mage looked like an eagle forced into a man suit, with his hooked nose and feathery hair.

"Very well done, Ms Edstow. Your phrasing is impeccable. Although perhaps next time you could focus upon incantations that provide a measurable result?"

Reetha flushed again and bent her head down. Her curtain of silvery blond hair swept forward to obscure her face and embarrassment from view. Jyx fought the urge to snort. Her phrasing was substandard and she'd copied the incantation structure from *Fforde's Guide to Manifestation.*

"Well, class. On the whole, you produced some solid work. Very good foundations for this semester," Professor Tourney said. "However, at least three of you need to work very hard. I am disturbed by the outcomes of your incantations."

He hauled himself to his feet, gripping the handle of his cane with claw-like hands. Three students stared at their desks, trying to ignore the multi-coloured frogs hopping around the floor—frogs which, in a perfect world, would have been robins. They had got it wrong but at least they made something happen, unlike Reetha, thought Jyx as he glared at the back of Reetha's head.

"I recommend that you each study chapters two and three of *Fforde's*, although it is advisable that you do not copy his incantations exactly. It is important that you read and understand what you see. Do not skip the important phrases, but you must also include your personal clauses. This is what will ensure success."

The professor waved his hands around as he talked, punctuating each sentence with a finger poke aimed at the ceiling. Jyx smirked. At least the professor had noticed what Reetha had done.

"What about your book, professor?" Reetha asked.

"I would also recommend that you study my book, yes. This is not mindless self-promotion. This is simple fact. I am not a professor of incantations for nothing, no? While you are discussing these things over lunch, you may wish to speak to Jyximus Faire. He clearly has a head for this subject."

Jyx started at the mention of his name, but his surprise spread across his face as a smile. Professor Tourney never complimented anyone. If he didn't find the class too basic for his abilities, he would have been proud.

The professor hauled the door open and swept out of the classroom. The students erupted into chatter as they gathered their books. Several shot envious looks in Jyx's direction. He ignored them. The highborn students would never confront him openly, not a scholarship student from the Underground City. Markus ignored their contempt and hung back with Jyx.

"Jyx, why are you reading about earth magick?"

"Because I can." Jyx swept the two books into his satchel. He'd need to take back the earth magick book, but he couldn't decide if he should notify the librarian about the missing pages. He wasn't authorised to take the book out until next year, but if another student reported the damage, the librarian might run one of her charms and find out Jyx was the last person to read it.

"But it's not on this year's syllabus."

"So? I understand it now. Why should I wait until next year to study it?" Jyx looked past Markus, trying to spot Missa. She threw an apologetic glance over her shoulder as her friends swept her out of the room.

"But where did you get it?" Markus asked.

"It's amazing what you can find in the library. You should try it some time."

Jyx hurried away from Markus, heading into the corridor. A stream of students clattered past the classroom, and Jyx tagged along with the crowd. Yes, it truly was amazing what you could find in the library, and he knew exactly what to look for that night.

CHAPTER 3

Darkness surrounded him when he awoke with a start. Jyx tried to stretch but his fingers met cold, smooth oak. He couldn't stretch his legs either, as his feet pressed up against something solid. Jyx tried to roll over but wood met him on every side. Panic seized him like a leathery hand around his throat. Madame Snytches was known to lock errant students in the chest in her office. Was this the infamous chest? Had Markus turned evidence on him and given him up?

Jyx scrabbled at his wooden tomb until he could wriggle onto his side, legs tucked behind him and arms across his chest. He explored the wall in front of him with his fingers until he found a crack. The panicked hand loosened its grip on his throat. He worked his nails along the crack until he found a keyhole.

The memory clattered through his brain, dragging wakefulness behind it. He wasn't imprisoned in a chest. He was hiding. Jyx had climbed into the empty cabinet in the library and drawn the doors closed behind him. He must have fallen asleep waiting for the librarians to leave. Their mindless chatter had invaded his thoughts and made him dream of dancing teacups.

He opened the cabinet door a crack and pressed his face up to the narrow opening. The library lay beyond, spread out in silence like a banquet of knowledge awaiting hungry guests. Moonlight streamed through the stained glass windows, painting vivid pictures across the flagstone floor. Only the gentle tick of the ornate grandfather clock disturbed the peace.

Jyx pushed the door, slithered out of his hiding place, and sprawled across the floor. He rolled onto his back and seized his numb legs, digging his nails into the muscles to spark life into his limbs. Spikes of pain flared in his calves as feeling returned, and he hauled himself upright using the cabinet. He closed the door and drew a sigil over the lock. The librarians would continue to believe the cabinet to be out of use, leaving it empty for his nocturnal excursions into the archives.

The spiral staircase lay on the other side of the vaulted room. Jyx bent down to pull off his boots, and padded across the floor in his stockinged feet. The staircase stood beside the window that depicted the virtues of diligence and quiet reflection. Jyx suppressed a snort. If he stuck to those, he wouldn't be sneaking around the library at night, and he certainly wouldn't be working on next year's textbooks while topping all of this year's classes.

The worn stone steps led up to the narrow gallery that clung to the walls above the stacks. During the day, a fearsome Wolfkin barred access to the staircase, and only those with a signed and stamped permit could pass. Even the students with permits were terrified of the massive guardian, a muscled warrior with the head of a wolf. At night, the Wolfkin slept curled like a puppy in a wicker basket, its armour propped up against the bookshelves. Jyx dipped a hand into the pouch hanging from his belt, and withdrew a fistful of sleeping dust. The high mages in the Autumn Gloaming made the best powder, but he'd made do with cheap sand and geo magick sigils. Jyx blew the dust across the Wolfkin. It stirred once and began to snore.

Jyx stole up the staircase. The librarians kept their most dangerous or valuable texts in the gallery. Some of the books were so treacherous they were bound shut with powerful enchantments even Jyx couldn't unravel. Others were simply rare, and stored inside glass boxes on the shelves. The book Jyx sought was neither dangerous nor rare—simply reserved for more advanced students.

The *Dominantur Umbras* nestled between two ancient books bound in dragon skin. Jyx worked his fingers between the books and slid the *Dominantur* free, careful not to yank its spine or break its binding. Dark phantoms twisted within the depths of its slate-grey cover, its name a smudge of gold in the darkness. A double frisson of trepidation and excitement fluttered along Jyx's soul. This was shadow magick, only a hop, skip and a jump away from the darkest magicks of all.

At his touch, the cover flipped open. A pale lavender square of parchment clung to the title page. Jyx recognised the flowing script of the warning as the handwriting of Madame Snytches.

The Dominantur Umbras is reserved for students in the fourth year or higher, and should be issued only to those students believed to be responsible and mature. The Academy accepts no responsibility for loss or injury sustained following the use of this text.

Being caught with the book would definitely lead to a night in the notorious chest and Jyx shuddered. He flicked past the warning to the introduction. Densely packed text described the principles of shadow theft, enslavement and proper maintenance. Theft didn't concern him. There were plenty of unscrupulous traders in the Underground City who would give up their shadows for a few coins, and shadow slaves would make his mother's household chores a lot easier. Maybe he could sell them and earn a few coins himself.

Jyx closed the *Dominantur* and slid the book into his satchel, pre-lined with a square of blanket from his bed at home. He wouldn't be able to read the book at home; taking it out of the Academy would set off all kinds of alarms, and he'd probably lose his library privileges altogether.

Nothing stopping me reading this in here, though.

He patted his bag and headed back towards the spiral staircase. He'd told his mother he would be staying with Markus Prady tonight, knowing she would never dare breach the class boundaries between families to check up on him. He'd be able to study all night.

The Wolfkin stirred as he passed, and Jyx hurried across the library towards the reading area on the far side of the room. Tall bookshelves filled to groaning point with ancient tomes screened the reading area from the rest of the library. Jyx chose a table in the corner, and settled into the overstuffed chair. He pulled his parchment and quill from his satchel, flipped open the *Dominantur*, and began to read.

* * * *

A raven sat on the sill, peering through the window at the rebellious student. It knew the type; it had seen that thirsty expression before. It never ended well.

The raven took flight, bearing news of Jyx's transgression to a higher authority.

* * * *

Jyx walked along the corridor in the direction of his Sigils class. The taste of bacon lingered on his tongue, and he licked the last of the coffee from his lips. The canteen staff only allowed students one cup of the hallowed drink at breakfast, but Jyx's bleary eyes had convinced one of the nicer servers to give him a second. Jyx stifled a yawn and considered the possibility that Madam Edifer might notice his tiredness.

Still, the night spent reading the *Dominantur* had been worth it. The sheaf of papers in his satchel held copious notes, and while parts of the text proved dense or difficult, Jyx thought he'd understood most of it. He'd even managed to snare the tiny shadow of a moth that had blundered into the library, only setting it free just before he left. The book proved so engrossing he had barely noticed the sun come up, and he'd managed to return the book to the gallery and slip out of the library with only seconds to spare. He'd had to pretend to adjust his bootlaces outside the door to explain his presence to the librarians that morning.

"Jyximus Faire?"

Jyx stopped. A gnome stood in the corridor before him, flanked by a Wolfkin. The guard glared at him, yellow eyes burning in its wolfish face. The black fur of its canine head gave way to smooth black skin, encased in Academy armour. The gnome wore the royal blue robes of Administration, and Jyx recognised the emblem of the Academy's dean at his collar.

"Yes?"

"Dean Whittaker wishes to see you." The gnome turned to walk away, content that his statement would be taken as an order, rather than a request.

"Why?"

"If you come with us, you'll find out." The gnome cast a baleful glare over his shoulder.

The gnome led Jyx away from the main corridor into a wide passage to their left. Ancient tapestries covered the walls, depicting different scenes within magickal history. As with most stories told of battles or struggles, the illustrated events didn't agree with each other, depending on who produced them. The staff used them as an example to students to never accept anything blindly, but to always seek further knowledge. As much as he hoped it would, Jyx didn't think this maxim would help much if his nocturnal library visits were discovered.

Dean Whittaker's office lay at the centre of a labyrinth of passages, designed to prevent all but the most necessary excursions to intrude on his time. A massive oak door swung inwards, and the gnome scampered through, the slapping of his bare feet on stone arrested by the sudden appearance of carpet. The Wolfkin nudged Jyx forward and he stumbled into the room.

Bookcases lined every wall, and magickal apparatus covered every available flat space. Dean Whittaker did not tend towards modesty or minimalism. He wanted to display all he knew and all he owned. Jyx gazed at the books, his fingers itching to pry one free of its shelf. He could only dream of their contents.

Dean Whittaker sat in a large, high-backed chair beyond a vast, ebony desk. Magickal symbols made of mother-of-pearl were inlaid in the desk's surface, and a large phoenix feather quill lay on the blotter in front of the dean. He gestured to the empty seat across the desk. Jyx hesitated, and felt the Wolfkin's clawed hand land on his right shoulder. The guard propelled Jyx forward and pushed him down into the seat. Jyx straightened his robes and tossed an indignant look at the Wolfkin.

"Jyximus Faire. How nice to see you."

Dean Whittaker sat back in his tall chair. Jyx forced himself to make eye contact with the dean, but shudders ran down his spine to see the dancing flames in the dean's empty sockets. Jyx didn't even want to think about how the dean would actually "see" him.

"Dean Whittaker."

"I'm a very busy man, Mr Faire, so I'll get to the point. I'm assuming you're wondering why you've been called to my office?"

The dean steepled his fingers, his white skin stretched taut across his knuckles.

Jyx swallowed hard. "The thought did cross my mind, sir."

Jyx's mind fluttered from the geo magick book in his satchel, to the stolen hours with the *Dominantur Umbras* the night before. He risked a sideways glance at the Wolfkin behind him. He didn't think it was the same one from the library, but he couldn't be sure.

"We have a lot of students at the Academy, Mr Faire. Many of them pay good money to be here. Several of them perform to an exceptional standard, yourself included. Have no fear, we're aware of your abilities, but standards are what this Academy is founded upon. Do you understand?"

Jyx nodded but a cold slug of fear crawled down his spine. He resisted the urge to sniff his fingers, convinced the smell of ancient book dust on his hands would give him away. He didn't think the dean's sunken nose would smell it, but the Wolfkin certainly would.

"Of course you do. You're a bright boy. Almost too bright, one might say. I am well aware that you feel we are holding you back."

The flames in the dean's eyes burned slightly colder than before. Jyx wriggled in the seat until a clawed hand clamped down on his shoulder. He forced himself to look at the dean, convinced that his ears had turned an unpleasant shade of red.

"Wh-what makes you say that, sir?"

"The fact that you hide advanced textbooks in your satchel, which you even have the temerity to read in class, and the fact that you regularly sneak into the library after hours to read texts which are often beyond the level of some of this Academy's professors, let alone your classmates. Never mind the declarations, Mr Faire, I know about it all."

The dean waved away Jyx's unspoken protests of innocence. His stomach churned as he thought about what would come next. Suspension? Expulsion? Worse? It would kill his mother if he were kicked out of the Academy. Jyx tried not to gasp when he thought of leaving the Academy and its delicious library behind. He couldn't

THE NECROMANCER'S APPRENTICE

stomach the idea of going to one of the institutions in the Underground City.

"Your line of thinking is correct, Mr Faire. Normally such transgressions would be punishable with expulsion. There is a reason that we keep you at a certain level. We need to be sure that you are mature enough to handle the magick to which we grant you access." The dean's expression softened, and warmth crept back into the flames in his eyes. Jyx continued to stare, panic gripping and squeezing his stomach. Acid burned at the back of his throat as he fought to control his thoughts. Telepathy on students was supposed to be forbidden.

"Wh-what will you do?"

"Mr Faire, you are an exceptional student. The very fact that you have been able to study this magick, and understand it for the most part, tells me that you have sought this knowledge not out of arrogance, but simply impatience. Perhaps there is something I can do to remedy this yearning of yours."

The dean snapped his fingers and the Wolfkin released its grip on Jyx's shoulder. It stomped across the dean's office and opened a door behind the desk. The door was set flush in the smooth wooden panelling of the wall and Jyx hadn't noticed it when he first entered the office. A tall woman, taller even than the dean, swept into the office. She wore jet-black robes, devoid of any markings or devices, and a yellow bone held a pile of black hair on top of her head. She might have been beautiful if her features hadn't been so severe. A raven sat on her right shoulder.

"Your Excellency," the dean said.

He rose and bowed to the newcomer. She waved him away and sat in his chair. The dean stood several feet behind, his eyes fixed on the floor. Jyx stared at the woman, unsure as to whether he should stand in greeting. "Excellency" implied someone of rank—many more ranks above the dean.

"Jyximus Faire, I presume?"

The woman didn't so much look at him as through him. Her pale blue eyes reminded Jyx of the wolves in the City Zoological Gardens. Her stare carried the weight of the ages, and Jyx gripped the arms of his chair, convinced he would suffocate if he maintained eye contact.

"Y-yes."

"Good. I am Eufame Delsenza."

Jyx jerked in his seat and stared at the dean, searching for confirmation of her words. The necromancer general was here, in the Academy? The dean gave a tiny nod, and focused his attention on a spot on the floor.

"You've heard of me. Good. Then you know that I have been recently hired for a rather large job." Eufame's voice skated along the edge of a razor—buzzing decay on one side, and frozen winter on the other.

"The coronation."

"Indeed. Our illustrious boy prince is to become king, and he has a somewhat fanciful notion that the best way to cement the commencement of his rule is by parading around his ancestors as performing monkeys."

No one spoke ill of the royal family, not publicly, at least. Besides, Jyx thought the new king's idea was marvellous. What better way to announce you were now in charge than by having the whole royal line present at the coronation? He was surprised no one had ever thought of it before.

"Oh, close your mouth, boy. I speak as I find, and if you're to be my apprentice, you shall have to get used to that fact."

"Your apprentice?"

"Yes. My little friend here has been observing you for some time, and I was particularly impressed by your choice of text last night." Eufame gestured to the raven. Jyx couldn't swear to it, but he was sure it nodded at him. Was it the same raven from the canals? "The *Dominantur Umbras* is fascinating stuff, is it not?"

"It is, ma'am. I really enjoyed it."

"Please, call me Miss Delsenza. *Ma'am* is reserved for old people."

Jyx frowned. His mother had told him terror stories of Eufame Delsenza when he was little. She was at least four hundred years old, and she'd held the position of necromancer general for the past three hundred of those. The overcrowding in the graveyards in the Underground City made fears around the necromancer legendary. No one wanted to be one of her "experiments".

"Why have you been watching me?" Questions flooded his mind but Jyx forced himself to ask something relevant.

"My last apprentice didn't work out. I've needed a new one for some time but as I'm sure you can appreciate, I can't simply hire the first person I find. The dean here has been gracious enough to help me in the past. I normally wouldn't look at anyone below a fourth year but I think you could do well."

"I'd have to drop out of the Academy?"

"Yes, Jyx, you would, but I'm offering you an apprenticeship within the House of the Long Dead. Do you know what that could lead to?"

Jyx shook his head.

"Well, your prospects, should you remain here, are essentially restricted to freelance work, unless you choose to enter one of the conglomerates and work in their alchemical divisions. But I'm sure I don't need to remind you that the House of the Long Dead is attached to the City Archives, and we have links with the Mages of the Autumn Gloaming..."

Eufame left the words, and their promise, hanging in the still air of the dean's office. Jyx smiled, thinking of all the knowledge just waiting to be explored. Even better, a position with the necromancer general herself would have to lead to some kind of new accommodation for his family. Perhaps they could finally leave the Underground City. A tiny voice in the back of his head voiced caution, but Jyx stifled it beneath excitement at the prospect of seeing the City Archives.

All that knowledge had to be worth the risk of working for the necromancer general.

"I'll do it."

"Excellent. I knew you'd accept."

Eufame stood and swept across the room. The dean still refused to make eye contact. She'd almost reached the door by the time Jyx found his voice.

"How did you know I'd say yes?"

"Because you'd be a fool not to."

CHAPTER 4

The carriage rattled along the cobbled avenue towards the House of the Long Dead, which stood on the outskirts of the Upper City, next door to the vast Necropolis. Jyx stared out of the window as several miles of graveyard slipped past. He tried to pick out details but one broken headstone looked much like another.

"The only thing older than the Necropolis is the Palace," Eufame said. She sat beside him, but Jyx couldn't see her face in the depths of her hood.

"I've never seen it before."

"Dean Whittaker leads me to believe your family resides in the Underground City?"

"That's right. My mother and my brothers and sisters live on Benefactor's Close. I wasn't allowed to tell my mother the good news."

Jyx scowled. Dean Whittaker's insistence that he leave the Academy immediately rather soured his excitement at being chosen as Eufame's new apprentice.

"Dean Whittaker has about as much emotion as my left boot, which is ironic since I know he says the same about me. No matter. I will have a note sent to your family to explain your new position, as I imagine your mother may worry when you do not return home this evening. If you pass your probationary period, then you can invite them to stay in one of our residences."

"One of..."

"Of course, Jyx. We have several residences. You yourself will stay with me, but I have properties all over the city. I am sure your siblings would love the open spaces out at Marsh House."

"You'd really let all of them live there?"

"Indeed. The apprentice of the necromancer general holds a higher station than an Academy student, and it really wouldn't do for his family to be holed up in a dingy tenement in the Underground City."

Jyx thought he heard laughter at the edges of Eufame's tone, but said nothing in reply. He didn't want to risk her withdrawing her offer. He hoped she would let him write the note to his family himself. His mother would have to fetch one of the judges to read it, but she'd recognise his handwriting all the same.

A large building shimmered into view through the afternoon heat haze. It crouched beside the Necropolis like a panther waiting to pounce, all black marble and Gothic arches. Stained glass windows studded its sleek exterior, and gargoyles topped the towers that punctured the clear blue sky. Its shining wall reflected an image of the Necropolis, sending the image of the cemetery into infinity.

The carriage bounced along the cobbles alongside the behemoth of a building and turned left onto a paved road. They passed under an arch between two massive statues of jackal-headed men, and pulled into a circular courtyard. A fountain took centre stage in the yard, cast in black wrought iron and surrounded by black marble. Dark red liquid played where Jyx expected to see water.

"That isn't blood. It's just coloured to look like it," Eufame said, noticing Jyx's pained expression as she turned to look at him.

"Why?"

"People expect a certain visual aesthetic to the House of the Long Dead. We like to give them what they want. Besides, we find it amusing. And, by 'we', I mean that I find it amusing."

Jyx looked away, unable to decide which was the more frightening—the blood-red fountain, or Eufame's attempt at a smile.

The carriage door opened, and a white-skinned Wolfkin clad in the black robes of the House appeared. It held open the door as Eufame stepped down into the courtyard. Jyx tried to emulate her smooth grace, but his foot caught the hem of his robe and he tumbled down the steps on his bottom. Eufame didn't notice, and strode away across the yard. The Wolfkin seized

Jyx's collar and yanked him upright, gesturing for him to follow.

Jyx trotted after Eufame, conscious of the sheer scale of the house. The building rose for several storeys above him, each stained glass window separated by more statues. He recognised some of the ancient deities from his clandestine readings, but some of the figures both confused and repulsed him. He knew the house practiced arcane magick and dealt with beings far older than those the Academy would recognise, but Jyx gulped. For the first time since the age of six, the age he first discovered he could command the cold ashes in the fireplace, he felt out of his depth.

A gathering of men clustered near the doorway. One of them held the reins of an imposing horse, its bronze coat dull in the shadow cast by the building, while another held a vast bouquet of glass flowers. Hope and expectation lit up their faces when they saw Eufame. A short man with the shaved head of a cleric stepped forward, his robes of state flapping around his ankles.

"Miss Delsenza! We have awaited your arrival—"

"Save your breath, Dumier. I am uninterested and unmoved by your offers. You may tell Berelsine the same thing so that he may cease sending you cretins to harass me." Eufame twisted her lips into a snarl, echoed in the low growl of the Wolfkin at her side.

"But Miss Delsenza!"

Eufame turned on her heel and strode up the

wide staircase towards a tall set of doors. Scarlet flames blazed in braziers either side of the doors, yet Jyx felt no warmth as he passed. He shuddered as he crossed the threshold, aware that a pair of Wolfkin guarded the doorway on the inside.

"Who were they?" Jyx looked back towards the door. The cluster of men jostled for position, peering through the gap between the doors as they swung shut.

"Suitors, Jyx."

"Marriage suitors?" Jyx looked at Eufame, trying to envision a man who would want to marry such a forbidding woman. She was so different from his warm, round mother. Jyx couldn't imagine Eufame bending over a cauldron of nourishing broth, or cradling a sleeping child with one arm while bouncing a toddler on her knee.

"What else? However, city law prevents a married woman from holding any form of high office." Eufame peeled her long gloves from her hands and dropped them into a waiting bowl held by a grovelling servant. The little man scurried away towards a small doorway.

"So you'd have to give up your job?"

"Being necromancer general is not simply a job, Jyx. It's a vocation, and one at which I happen to be very good. No, none of those men out there actually wish to marry me. That silly old fool over at the Hall of Records wants my position and keeps paying suitors to try to entice me. Although I rather suspect the idea was not his own. There are others who would see me out of office." Eufame glared at the doors as if her very stare could penetrate the thick wood. Jyx wouldn't be entirely surprised if it did.

He stood away from the door, one foot in the pool of light thrown onto the floor by the brazier. Jyx looked around the atrium, aware that none of his fellow Academy students even knew what the house looked like. Some of them even disbelieved its very existence. Several storeys above them, light passed through the stained panes of a glass dome, throwing flashes of colour across the marble floor. Paintings of jackal-headed men covered the walls, and a band of glyphs ran around the room at head height. Jyx couldn't read the language.

"Anyway, Jyx, enough of such unpleasantries. Welcome to the House of the Long Dead! This is our entrance hall, but I expect you figured that part out for yourself." Eufame gestured to the square, lofty room.

"Whereabouts is it that you work, Miss Delsenza?"

"Downstairs. That's where the magick happens. The upper chambers are mostly residential, administrative, or for entertaining."

"Entertaining?"

"Yes. Strange as it may seem, we host the occasional formal gathering here, as well as a few informal get-togethers. We hold a lot of cultural cache with the government, and we have a lot of visiting scholars. Once you've been here a while and you're used to my way of working, I'll take you to the archives."

"Visiting scholars?"

"Yes. We hold an awful lot of knowledge within our walls. But it'll be a while before you'll get to see them. Or the archives. There will be no midnight excursions to peruse our books. Do you understand?"

"Yes." Jyx nodded, more interested in the strange wall paintings.

"I mean it, Master Faire. At the Academy, the worst punishment you could face would be expulsion. Well, you're not at the Academy anymore."

Jyx followed Eufame's gaze across the entrance hall. Streaks of white disrupted the smooth black marble of the floor at the bottom of the grand staircase. Eufame made a dismissive gesture with her bony fingers. Jyx crossed the hall, an inexplicable ball of dread growing in his stomach. He reached the white streaks and gasped. A skeleton was embedded in the floor. He looked back at Eufame, searching her face for answers. A smirk hovered around her mouth.

"Meet the last apprentice who disobeyed my orders."

Jyx stared at Eufame. The necromancer general looked at the skeleton and back at Jyx. Her pointed eyebrow mirrored the arched window behind her.

A paw planted firmly in between Jyx's shoulders. The Wolfkin shoved him across the hall. Eufame turned and headed for a wide doorway set into the wall. A jackal head sculpture protruded from the door arch, its mouth open in a roar. Or a scream—Jyx couldn't tell which.

"Come along, Jyx. You knew life here would be different. Do as I say, learn well and work hard, and you'll be fine. You've shown a lot of promise so far."

Eufame snapped her fingers and the door swung inwards. Jyx watched her disappear into the gloom beyond and gulped. He glanced back at the main entrance, guarded by the twin Wolfkin. Another shove in his back sent him stumbling towards the door.

A stone spiral staircase led into suffocating gloom. Jyx clung to the handrail on the way down, conscious of the Wolfkin behind him, and the skeleton set into marble upstairs.

"Come along, Jyx. Don't dawdle on your first day." Eufame's voice echoed up the stairwell, hollow reverberations against cold stone. Jyx couldn't decide if the harsh edge to her tone was admonishment or amusement.

Jyx stumbled as he reached the bottom of the staircase. Purple flames burned in braziers on each wall in the tiny anteroom. Figures, painted flat in profile, cavorted in narrow bands across the walls. A pair of giant Wolfkin portraits adorned the wall either side of the archway opposite the staircase. Jyx assumed they were Wolfkin—they had the same canine heads and muscular human bodies. Yet unlike the Wolfkin behind him, the figures wore elaborate headdresses and simple loincloths instead of the armour favoured by Eufame's guards.

The Wolfkin behind him shoved him towards the arch. A blast of cold air hit Jyx in the face when he stepped through into the vaulted room beyond. The room stretched far away into the gloom, and more braziers flickered from the columns holding the vaulted ribs aloft. A gallery ran around the Vault near the ceiling, granting access to the glass cabinets of potions and salves that lined the walls. Doorways were hewn into the stone walls, the rooms beyond cold and dark. Jyx stared into the empty portal to his right, and imagined what could lurk in the depths of its shadows.

"Welcome to the Vault."

Eufame stood before him, and gestured to the cavernous room. More painted figures adorned the walls below the gallery, interspersed with the same strange glyphs Jyx had seen upstairs. A narrow table stretched along one wall, groaning beneath the weight of glass vials and tubes. Braziers burned beneath some of the flasks, giving off coloured smoke and intoxicating fumes.

"Is this where you work?" Jyx stared at the apparatus. The only time he'd seen a set-up like that was an engraving in a dusty book about alchemy.

"It is, yes. The House of the Long Dead occupies far more space than the building above you. Admin and entertaining happens upstairs, but we do all of the actual work down here in the Vault for containment purposes. As you can tell, it's a lot colder down here, but it makes it easier to work our magick on the bodies. That, and it stops them decaying before we can finish our work," Eufame replied.

She strode away from Jyx. Bandaged bodies lay on marble slabs on either side of the room's central aisle. Jyx shuddered, unable to remember the last time he'd been close to a dead body. Living in the Underground City, he'd encountered many suspicious piles at the bottom of the many closes, and seen the apprentice undertakers with their dead-carts, heading for the graveyards, but these were real corpses, and royal ones, at that.

"You'll soon grow accustomed to this," Eufame said.

Jyx scowled in her direction. He hated how easily she seemed to read his thoughts. Perhaps he'd find a text in the archives that might teach him to guard his mind. Eufame's step faltered and Jyx thought of his mother, scrubbing the kitchen floor with black soap. He wouldn't even be able to consider pursuing knowledge unless Eufame felt he needed to learn it.

A tabby cat poked its head around the side of the tomb nearest to Jyx. It peered up at him with huge golden eyes, its whiskers quivering in the cold air. The Wolfkin behind Jyx uttered a low growl, but the cat ignored it. Jyx thought of the rat catchers in the Underground City, huge fierce bags of fur with claws like knives and tempers to match. The little tabby barely seemed related to them.

"You have a cat?"

"I do. Meet Bastet. She keeps down the rodents in here. She's quite friendly, I assure you. Nothing like the beasts you'll be used to. Now come along, Jyx. I must show you your quarters before I can set you any tasks. It's vital that you consider this place to be your home."

Jyx trotted down the central aisle that ran the length of the room. Eufame paused, and Jyx saw that another aisle crossed his path, cutting through the slabs across the width of the Vault. From this vantage point, the far end of the room's dim lines was faintly discernible in the gloom. More bubbling apparatus occupied a far wall, though the smells from those flasks were less pleasing to his nose. Tall archways cut the walls at either end of the shorter aisle, and Wolfkin paintings guarded the doors. The more he stared at the paintings, the more Jyx became convinced that they were not Wolfkin. Perhaps they're Wolfkin ancestors.

"Jyx, you're staring a lot. It is most unbecoming," Eufame said.

"It's all just so new to me," Jyx replied.

"I understand that, but before we go much further, I feel I must point out to you that the world is a lot older than you realise. The magick you learned in the Academy is useful, yes, but there are far more ancient, far more powerful forms of magick. If you learn well, then I will be able to teach you these. But you must understand that the ways of this house are not the ways of your previous life."

"I know things will be different. I don't have to put up with that idiot Markus Prady, for one thing," Jyx said.

"That is true, but things will be different in other ways too. You already know that I am older than most. I was five hundred and seventy-three on my last birthday. My age alone grants me access to magick beyond that which the Academy will even officially recognise. You have become part of a very ancient tradition, Jyx."

Jyx stared at Eufame. He wanted to see lines on her face, or streaks of white in her mane of black hair. He knew she was old, but hearing her say it unsettled him. He wanted to run away, leaving nothing behind but his screams, but a voice whispered in the back of his mind. It was the same voice that persuaded him to seek out forbidden texts in the library, and told him to accept Eufame's offer. The same voice that sought knowledge—at any price.

"Few can accept my age, not least the fools that run this city. Did you know that I originally embalmed most of these royal buffoons that the prince hopes to present as part of his coronation pageant?"

"Really?" Jyx fought to banish the gawp from his face. He didn't want Eufame to think he was surprised by everything.

"Yes, Jyx, I embalmed them. You see, the necromancer general does not merely raise the dead. It is part of our job to prepare and protect them. That was the role of the Wolfkin for two millennia, before the Academy started using them as guard dogs, and this house was established."

The Wolfkin behind Jyx growled. Jyx turned and looked up into its canine face. Sleek grey fur gave way to smooth grey skin that rippled across huge muscles. Its lips vibrated with the snarl, displaying glimpses of white fang. Jyx knew he should be afraid, but he saw pride and disgust in the Wolfkin's icy blue eyes. The growl was not intended for him.

"But the Wolfkin—"

"You will learn of their ancestry when they deem it to be necessary. It is not my story to tell, but theirs. Anyway, enough of that lesson." Eufame clapped her hands and wiggled her fingers, as if trying to dispel negative vibes.

"So the rooms..."

"Yes. The Vault's layout is rather simple. The doorway in the western wall leads to my chambers. Do you know why the west is significant?" Eufame pointed to the doorway at the far end of the short aisle.

"I've never come across anything about directions in my reading," Jyx said.

His ears burned and he stared at the floor, cursing himself for disregarding all of the work on folklore. *I just wanted to learn the magick.*

"A common mistake, Jyx. People dismiss folklore or myth as trivial or silly. They forget it contains nuggets of truth. In this case, the west is important as the direction in which the sun sets. The Lands of the Dead lie to the west. It seems fitting that my chambers would lie to the west, doesn't it?"

Jyx nodded.

"On no account are you to venture beyond that arch. If you require me and I am not in the Vault, one of the Wolfkin will fetch me. You may also ask Bastet to find me. You, however, may not."

"Yes, Miss Delsenza."

"Your chambers are this way."

Eufame ducked beneath the archway in the eastern wall. Jyx gulped to see the darkness swallow her up. He forced himself to ignore the rising sense of dread, and plunged headfirst into the black shadows beyond the archway.

CHAPTER 5

Two chambers lay beyond the archway, connected by doorways cut into the stone. Empty bookcases lined the walls of the first room, surrounding the fireplace in the southern wall. Jyx looked at the cold grate, and pictured flames dancing, casting their shadows across the floor. The fireplace was the first sign of real habitation in the house, and his heart leapt when he spotted a basket of firewood on the floor nearby.

"This will become your study as you become more adept. Each worker at the house collects their own library, and you will be expected to fill books with your observations and thoughts about all that you see and do. Supplies will be provided and if you work well, one day your own books will line these shelves," said Eufame, gesturing to the bookcases. Jyx gasped at the idea that this would be his library, a collection of his very own.

"Indeed, Jyx. I also see you noticed the firewood. Feel free to light a fire should you choose to. I do not share your specific set of needs, but they will be catered to during your time here."

The Wolfkin grunted and pointed at a velvet curtain in the corner. It crossed the room and lifted the swathe of fabric to reveal a large box. A ring of felt surrounded the hole in the top of the box, and a wooden rod hung from the ceiling on a length of chain. Eufame wrinkled her nose at the sight of it.

"That is the garderobe. I am given to understand that inhabitants of the Underground City deposit their waste into chamber pots, which are emptied out of the window. Is this correct?"

"Some people do. Some people have chutes in the house that lead to the sewers."

"I see. Well this garderobe is plumbed into the sewer system, so you need only pull that chain when you are done. I will not have the purity of this house infected with abjection."

Eufame swept out of the chamber and into the next room. Another fireplace took up part of a wall, back to back with its twin in the first room, and tapestries hung on the other walls. They depicted scenes of legend or myth, a far cry from the austere paintings on the walls elsewhere in the house. Mannequins in the corner held two changes of clothes, and an empty sarcophagus stood against the far wall.

"This will be your bedchamber. I received

these tapestries from the Academy in order to better ease your transition." Eufame pointed at the tapestries, although her downturned mouth and wrinkled nose suggested she didn't approve of their frivolous content.

"Bedchamber?" Jyx looked around, eager to see a bed. His small pallet at home would be nothing compared to whatever palatial furniture Eufame provided. Hopefully it would be free of the fleas that infested the garret of his Underground City tenement.

Eufame smirked and gestured to the sarcophagus. Jyx stared, horror rising in the back of his throat as he thought of the last person to rest there.

"Oh do not look so surprised, Jyx. Consider where you are, and remember that there are many who would willingly donate limbs in order to sleep in the resting place of a king."

"A king?"

"Yes. The great-great-great-great-grandfather of our brand new kingling, if I remember correctly. His dimensions most closely resemble yours, hence the choice of his coffin as your bed. Now come along, Jyx. We must get to work. These corpses will not raise themselves."

Eufame left the room, and Jyx trotted after her. The Wolfkin waited for them in Jyx's study, bringing up the rear as they headed back into the main Vault. Eufame walked along the central aisle towards the far end of the room, and stopped beside a red marble slab and its resident mummy. The bandages were dark yellow, spotted with brown, but a delicate diadem still encircled its skull.

"Meet Queen Neferpenthe. She's one of our oldest, and she's to be the jewel of the procession. She had magick of her own so we are to treat her very carefully."

"How old is she?" asked Jyx. He stared at the moonstone set into the diadem, resting on the mummy's forehead. The stone was larger than the crusts of bread he could expect for supper at home.

"I am unsure." Eufame's expression said otherwise but she clapped her hands and moved on. "Now how much do you know about necromancy?"

"Not as much as I'd like to. The Academy never talked about it, so I read bits and pieces in the library, but not all of it made sense, especially when I was translating things myself. Everyone acted like it was something we shouldn't even mention."

"That's hardly surprising. Necromancy is considered the darkest of all dark arts. It involves calling beyond the veil, and commanding the spirit back to its body. The process is relatively simple for the newly dead, and many are only too happy to return. But the longer the spirit and the body are apart, the more difficult it becomes," said Eufame.

"What do you need me to do?" asked Jyx. His mind flitted among the fragments of knowledge gleaned in the library. Perhaps Eufame would allow him to unwrap the mummy, or maybe he would be allowed to create the ritual circle.

"Sweep the floor."

The Wolfkin stepped forward and thrust a broom into Jyx's hand. Jyx stared down at the rough bristles and the handle worn smooth with use. It wasn't even the ritual broom used to sweep psychic negativity from the circle; it was just a regular broom.

"Don't look like that, Jyx. Everyone has to start somewhere. Now I suggest you start at the far end and make your way towards the spiral stairs."

Eufame turned her back on Jyx and leaned over the mummy on the slab. Jyx scowled and jabbed at the floor with the broom. A heavy paw landed on his shoulder and guided him across the Vault. A claw appeared at the edge of his vision and pointed at the corner. Jyx turned around and stared up into the impassive face of the Wolfkin. Beyond, Eufame busied herself with Queen Neferpenthe, sliding a thin blade between the ancient bandages. Jyx looked down. Dust covered the floor around the slabs, settled in the cracks between the flat stones.

I could use a whirlwind charm.

"Jyx, I know what you're thinking, but just use the broom," said Eufame, not even looking up.

Jyx threw an evil look in the necromancer general's direction, and stabbed at the floor with the broom.

CHAPTER 6

Jyx sat in his study in the new rocking chair Eufame had provided. After a week of menial tasks, she'd felt it only fair that Jyx receive some kind of reward. With no other form of seating in his quarters, the chair seemed the ideal choice, and after a day of menial tasks, rocking before a roaring fire was Jyx's sole point of pleasure. A single book had also been provided to start his new collection, a thin tome about ritual circles. It lay on the bookshelf, discarded once Jyx realised he'd already read it during an illicit browsing session in the Academy library between study periods. He glared at it and snorted—such juvenile material. Even Markus Prady could have understood it.

He felt guilty to suddenly think of Markus; he hadn't thought of his life before the house very often during his first week. Eufame's tasks consumed his time during the day, and at night he was so exhausted he fell into a dreamless sleep. Yet with the chair came parchment and a quill, and Eufame allowed him to compose a short note to his mother. Dean Whittaker had sent word about Jyx's removal to the house, but Jyx wanted to explain further himself. He was careful about what he said, knowing that a judge would be required to read the note to his mother, but he wanted her to know he was safe, and if everything went well, he'd finally be able to provide for them.

The note lay bound in a neat scroll on the fireplace, ready for delivery, and Jyx's study journal lay open in his lap. Eufame instructed him to keep one, making notes on all he saw and learned in the Vault. After a week, his scratchy handwriting covered just one page of the notebook. So far, all he'd seen Eufame do was unwrap several mummies, but she spoke to them in an alien tongue as she did so, and Jyx noted only snippets of what he thought she'd said. Without access to a library, Jyx had no hope of translating any of it—even if he'd known what language it was.

His single page of notes related to the task Eufame allowed him to do. Sweeping the entire Vault took two days, after which he spent another two days mopping the floor. His decision to separate the ordinary dust from the magickal dust earned him a rare smile from Eufame, and by day five, she allowed him to disenchant the piles of bandages retrieved from the mummies. A Wolfkin took away the remaining linen to be burned in the House's furnaces, while Jyx caught the enchantments in old glass bottles.

"Those enchantments may be reused, so we might as well keep them. It isn't exactly safe to burn enchanted fabric. One never knows which charm will activate a rogue fire elemental," Eufame had said.

She'd told him a tale about a previous apprentice who had done exactly that, and the ensuing flame plague almost destroyed half of the city. Jyx laughed at the requisite points of the story but he couldn't help hearing a vague warning behind Eufame's words. He spent the rest of the day storing the enchantment bottles in the cabinets up in the gallery.

He studied his notes, wondering what use he could find for this new skill. Perhaps he could disenchant the fabrics on sale in the Mystic Market, and sell the enchantments to the back street dealers of the Underground City. He tapped his quill against his lower lip, and frowned. There was a flaw in this plan—it required him to leave the House of the Long Dead, and Eufame didn't even allow him to leave the Vault.

Movement caught his attention by the door. A pair of eyes burned like golden droplets of fire in the pool of darkness near the arch. Jyx closed the notebook and set it on the floor with the quill. Bastet padded into the chamber, flicking her tail as she went. She stopped three feet away from the rocking chair, and sat.

"Hello, Bastet. What are you doing in here?"

She wiggled her whiskers in reply, swishing her tail across the flagstone floor. She caught sight of the pewter plate beside the fireplace, a plate that had, until recently, held Jyx's supper. The cat mewed, and Jyx tossed her a few morsels of chicken he'd saved from his meal. He'd never been in a position to have scraps to feed an animal before.

"Do you think Miss Delsenza would let me have a pet? I mean, I used to have my brothers and sisters to talk to at home. Well, I didn't talk to them much, if at all, but they were there if I wanted to talk to them. It's a bit, well, quiet here."

Bastet stretched, never taking her liquid eyes off Jyx.

"I suppose you're right. I'm still new here, and I doubt she'd let me have a pet in case it contaminated something. I just wish I had someone to talk to, or something to do."

Bastet looked at the bookshelf, and back at Jyx. He followed her gaze to the single book.

"I've already read it."

"Then read it again."

Jyx looked up to see Eufame framed by the archway. His cheeks burned with shame, and he wondered what she'd heard. He thought again of the skeleton embedded in the upstairs floor.

"Good evening, Miss Delsenza."

"Good evening, Jyx. I have been summoned to the Palace to give the prince a progress report, and I don't really have time for it, but he doesn't like to be kept waiting. However, I did take you on as an apprentice for a reason, so I was wondering if you'd care to expand your repertoire of chores?"

"Of course! What would you like me to do?" Jyx stood up, brushing the crumbs from his robe.

"There is a pot of salve in the Vault. I need you to anoint the eyelids of those mummies whom I have already unwrapped. The salve contains a particular compound that only the dead can see on the spiritual plane, and it will help guide them back to their body. It allows the dead to 'see', so to speak. Will you be able to manage that?"

"Of course, Miss Delsenza! What is the salve called?" Jyx snatched up his journal and quill, and dipped the pen into the inkwell on the mantelpiece.

"*Aperuit oculos.* If you have any concerns, then cease proceedings and ask me your questions when I return. If in doubt, do nothing. I would rather explain it again and use up more time than have you do it wrong. You don't have any incantations to worry about, or anything of that sort. Merely smear the salve onto the eyelids, and move onto the next one."

Jyx nodded, scribbling the name of the salve and a brief description of its use in his book.

"Then I shall bid you goodnight, Jyx. Do not wait up for me. I suspect I shall be some time. Bastet will remain here to keep you company, and there will be Wolfkin in the chambers upstairs should you require anything."

Eufame turned and melted into the darkness beyond the archway. Jyx hurried into his bedchamber to change back into his working robe, and almost ran into the Vault, eager to begin work. Bastet followed him through the Vault and sat on the floor beside the central aisle.

The salve sat on the slab at the farthest end of the chamber beside a tiny corpse. Stripped of its bandages and protective charms, the mummy seemed vulnerable and fragile, and Jyx suppressed a shudder to see its sunken stomach and shrivelled limbs.

"It's hard to believe this is royalty," said Jyx, looking at Bastet. She gazed back, impassive as ever.

He dipped a finger into the gooey salve, and held it up to his nose. It smelled strongly of violets and peppermint, with an undertone of something darker, and more sinister. Holding his breath, he smeared a thin film onto both eyelids of the mummy.

"Well that's one done. Hopefully he'll be able to find his body now," said Jyx.

He picked up the pot and moved onto the next slab, mindful of the cat watching him from the central aisle. Gazing down the Vault, he saw that Eufame had unwrapped half of the mummies already. He sighed, glancing at the doorway to his chambers.

I doubt I'll be getting much sleep tonight.

Still, this was a big responsibility, and Eufame had left him alone to do it.

Jyx anointed the next mummy. Perhaps this would be his big chance to prove his worth, and leave behind the housework she'd made him do so far.

CHAPTER 7

Without the sun to guide him, Jyx had little idea how much time had passed by the time he'd finished anointing the eyes of the unwrapped mummies. However, his week of chores and general mundane tedium taught him to measure time using the black candles set in heavy, freestanding candelabrum along the central aisle. Judging by the amount they'd burned down, anointing the eyes had taken Jyx around two hours.

"I suppose I can go to bed now." Jyx's voice disappeared into the depths of the Vault, swallowed by its emptiness. He expected to hear claws clicking on stone, for Bastet to appear around the side of one of the slabs, or perhaps for heavy paws to thud down the spiral staircase from the chambers above.

Jyx peered into the gloom of the Vault. No

Wolfkin glared at him from corners, and no cat loitered at his feet. For the first time since he'd arrived at the House, Jyx was entirely alone. His mind was free from Eufame's shackles.

I can think of whatever I want. Completely unbidden, his first liberated thought flitted through his mind, concerned entirely with Eufame's private library. The voice in the back of his mind tried to describe what dark wonders it might contain. One of the tomes was bound to contain details of the rituals she would be performing. If he were to read that, and more importantly understand it, then she might, just might, let him assist. No more sweeping. Better yet, his journal might become something worth keeping.

Another, more faint, voice tickled the back of his mind. It reminded him of the skeleton in the floor and Eufame's other warnings. Jyx ignored it, and crossed the Vault to duck through the archway into the darkness of Eufame's chambers. Braziers on the walls flared, casting electric blue sparks across the floor as the cobalt flames flickered into life. More mysterious paintings covered the walls, although these paintings were white lines inscribed onto the black stone. Jyx didn't recognise the figures, each of them painted with no considerations for perspective, their bodies face on, but their animal heads in profile.

The chamber seemed to be an atrium, with doorways to his left and right. A dark curtain hung across the wall in front of him. Jyx stared at the curtain but he couldn't decide on its colour as it shifted between deepest navy and violet. If he stared for too long, he swore he saw stars twinkling in its depths. The curtain called to him. It hid something, but in so doing, called attention to the fact there was something worth hiding. Jyx shook his head to break the curtain's hypnotic hold and crossed the room.

The curtain rippled like velvet beneath his fingers, and Jyx held his breath as he pushed it aside. A long vaulted room lay beyond, its high walls lined with shelves. More freestanding bookcases stood at random intervals, interspersed with tall granite statues. A warm glow suffused the room, but Jyx couldn't pinpoint its source. It seemed particularly focused over the massive statue of a man with the head of an ibis that dominated the centre of the room.

"All this knowledge...and Eufame knows the contents of all of these books?" Jyx couldn't help but speak aloud. An icy finger wriggled into his heart. How could he learn all of this? He certainly didn't have five hundred years ahead of him.

Or do I? If Eufame manages to keep herself young then why can't I?

Jyx turned to the wall to his left. The books on these shelves bore the most signs of wear, and held titles he felt he could read. He recognised the *Dominantur Umbras*, and several other tomes from the restricted section of the Academy's library. A slim volume, bound in bright green leather, caught his eye. The title, *Impetritae Inceptivus*, appeared in gold letters on the spine—*Initial Incantations*, if he'd translated it correctly.

The faint voice in the back of his head urged him to leave the book alone, to get out of the chamber and return to his own. The voice reminded him of the Wolfkin upstairs, and the ever-present Bastet. Jyx ignored it, telling himself that the missing cat and absent Wolfkin were a blessing. Surely Eufame would have left guards if she didn't think he could handle the contents of the library? Perhaps this was a test of some kind; she might even be disappointed if he didn't make a covert attempt to read something.

In the absence of tables or chairs, Jyx took the book to a nearby lectern. A small shelf on the stand held parchment and quills, and Jyx's heart leapt, shaking free the icy finger of fear. He could make notes and return the book before Eufame got back, and she'd never know. The voice in his mind reminded him of her eerie ability to read his thoughts, but excitement about the book in his hands suppressed any worry.

He leafed through its well-thumbed pages, careful not to pry apart those pages stuck together with stray candle wax or spirit gum. As expected, the book detailed the basic ritual circles required for necromancy, as well as the incantations he would need in order to call back the souls from beyond the Veil. The book advised caution, and listed a series of books for further reading, but Jyx ignored them all, too intent on copying down as much as he could.

Cramp attacked his hand after several pages of parchment, and Jyx glared at his painful fingers. *Still, I've made a lot of notes.* He padded across the library to return the book to the shelf, mindful to slide it back into its original slot. He gathered his sheets and made his way back to the curtain, casting a final gaze over his shoulder towards the books.

Jyx's ears pricked up at a noise out in the Vault. He strode across the atrium and peered out of the doorway into the gloom. A Wolfkin stood at the far end of the Vault, blocking the archway to the spiral staircase. It had its back to Jyx, communicating with something upstairs using a series of barks and growls. Jyx crouched low behind the slabs and hurried along the short aisle between Eufame's quarters and his own. The Wolfkin continued to pay him no attention, and Jyx leapt across the gap between the final slab and the doorway to his chambers.

The embers in Jyx's fireplace glowed in the darkness, burnt to almost nothing in his absence. Bastet lay curled up in his chair, her tail wrapped around her sleeping body. Keeping his eyes on her for fear she might wake, Jyx slid his illicit notes inside his journal on the shelf. Movement inside the Vault told him the Wolfkin's conversation had finished, and he slipped into his bedchamber.

"Ah, he's finished. Good boy. He might actually prove to be good at this." Eufame's voice echoed around the Vault. Jyx allowed himself a smile, convinced she would be even more impressed by his newfound knowledge.

Out in the vault, a Wolfkin barked in response.

"I know he is capable of overreaching himself but he learns quickly."

Another barked response.

"You misunderstand me, Kha. That's what I'm counting on."

* * * *

Jyx arose the next day, sure that Eufame would allow him to assist in some fundamental way. He ran through incantations in his head as he ate his breakfast, drawing sigils in the air with his spoon between mouthfuls of porridge.

"Jyx? Are you awake?"

Eufame's harsh tones drifted into his chamber. Jyx scraped the last of his porridge into his mouth, and deposited the bowl on the small table. It would disappear as mysteriously as it appeared. Not once in Jyx's week at the House had he seen any serving staff, but food continued to arrive, and plates disappeared, like clockwork.

Jyx strode into the Vault, his cloak flapping around his ankles. Eufame stood beside a mummy, her working knife in one hand and a length of ancient linen bandage in the other. She looked up and raised one eyebrow. Jyx's confident expression melted, dissolving into a pool of embarrassment as he tried not to trip over his robes.

"You've done a marvellous job with these mummies. Very even anointing." Eufame gestured to the mummies. Jyx beamed, the praise encouraging him to stand tall.

"Thank you. It was a great honour—"

"No it wasn't. It was a mundane chore. Don't try to pretend otherwise."

Eufame worked as she talked, sliding her knife beneath the wrappings of the mummy. She fished small charms and amulets from beneath the bandages, handing them to the Wolfkin standing behind her.

"Begging your pardon, but it was preferable to sweeping the floor."

Eufame straightened up and smiled, her silver lips curving into a predatory grin. Mirth sparkled in the depths of her cold eyes, and Jyx shuddered.

"So you do have a backbone! I was beginning to wonder. I rather suspect you'll do well at this, but only if you pace yourself. I trust you did some reading last night when you finished the anointing?"

Jyx nodded, unable to trust his voice to answer. He thought of the book about ritual circles, desperate not to think of *Impetritae Inceptivus*. Eufame bent back to her task, apparently satisfied with his answer.

"Excellent. If you proceed with the training I provide for you, then you'll do well, Jyx. The magick we do here isn't like the white nonsense you learn at the Academy. You can't race ahead when you're dealing with the sort of powers that we are. Do you understand?"

"Yes." Jyx forced himself to reply, his voice tight and unnatural. *She knows.*

"It will take me some time to unwrap the rest of these mummies, but you will be anointing their eyes again. Go to your chambers and study, and I shall call you when you're needed." Eufame waved her hand to dismiss him, and Jyx hurried across the Vault, trying not to trip over his feet in his haste to reach his chambers.

He snatched his study journal from the bookshelf and headed for his bedchamber. The addition of bedding made the empty sarcophagus more comfortable, and he crawled beneath the thick cloak donated by a Wolfkin from upstairs. He ignored the strong scent of dog and snuggled up to the thick fabric.

Jyx opened the journal and retrieved his loose notes, seemingly endless pages of cramped handwriting and careful sketches. So much knowledge was locked in these pages, even if they were only initial incantations. The temptation to commit them to memory tussled with his fear of discovery. Last night, Jyx felt sure Eufame would applaud his excursion into the forbidden library, but now, a serpent of dread settled its cold coils in the pit of his stomach. Perhaps he should burn the notes now, and be done with it.

Movement at the edge of his vision stirred Jyx from his thoughts. His own finger drew patterns in the air, patterns that he could only find in the pages scattered across his lap. His lips moved of their own accord, forming strange syllables and words without sound. Jolted into awareness, Jyx clamped his mouth shut and seized his hand from the cold air of the bedchamber.

"I can't help but learn new things," he whispered into the empty room.

He looked back down at the notes. Four pages lay face down to his left, while the remaining five lay face up. Four pages of incantations, sigils and ritual elements now burned in his brain, begging to be used.

"Jyximus!" Eufame's call resounded throughout the Vault.

Jyx shook his head, gathered the pages together, and stuffed them back into the study journal. He hid the book at the end of the sarcophagus beneath the sheets and straw mattress, and hurried back to the Vault.

"I've unwrapped some more mummies, Jyx. It makes sense for you to start anointing their eyes while I continue to work on the rest of them in this row." Eufame pointed to the mummies she'd unwrapped.

"Could I help unwrap them?" Jyx asked the question before he could stop himself. The incantations of unveiling and baring the flesh to the elements spun through his mind, determined to make their way out of his mouth.

"Not yet, Jyx. One step at a time, remember? Now if you don't mind doing the anointing—I have a surprise in store when you're finished."

Eufame returned to her work. Jyx trotted across the Vault to fetch the ointment. He smeared a thin layer across the eyelids of the first mummy, and his fingers fought to form the sigils required to open the eyes.

"Are you all right, Jyx?"

"Yes. Just cramp in my hands, that's all." Jyx allowed the lie to hang in the air, pretending to rub feeling back into his fingers. A Wolfkin emerged from the shadows to lurk behind him, and Bastet padded out from behind a nearby slab. Jyx forced his ill-gotten knowledge to the back of his mind, and pulled his focus to the jar of ointment in his hands.

It's going to be a long day, he thought as he moved to the next mummy.

CHAPTER 8

The black candles burned low as Jyx smeared ointment onto the cracked eyelids of the final mummy. Eufame stood behind him, her cold eyes warmed by her genuine appreciation of Jyx's work. Jyx straightened and rubbed at the stiffness in his lower back.

"Excellent. I was expecting this to take at least another day but this puts us ahead of schedule," said Eufame.

"And these are all royalty?" Jyx gazed the length of the Vault, trying to fathom how many members of the royal family he'd just anointed.

"Yes. Not all kings and queens per se but definitely part of the royal family at one time or another. The only ones we're missing are the prince's parents, uncles and grandparents, but they're in a different house."

"There's more than one house?"

Eufame nodded and strode away along the central aisle of the Vault. Jyx trotted to keep up with her, aware of Bastet padding along beside him. The Wolfkin remained in place by the doorway to the staircase. Apparently Eufame didn't feel she needed a continual guard.

"The two main houses are the Long Dead, which is this one, and the Near Dead, which houses the most recent mummies. It's next door to the palace, so people can continue to pay their respects. It always houses the two most recent generations," she said. Her voice echoed around the black stone walls.

"Are they necromancers too?"

"Not at all. The House of the Near Dead is staffed by embalmers and priests. They just prepare the bodies and manage visitors. It is forbidden to raise the near dead, so they don't need necromancers."

"Why is it forbidden?"

"Souls need time to adjust to the fact that they've passed over before they can be recalled. It would be cruel to pull them back to the corporeal realm before they had the time they needed. You'll learn more about it in time."

Eufame stopped at the entrance to her chambers. Jyx hung back, keen to stay away from the archway. He didn't want to demonstrate any prior knowledge of the rooms beyond the forbidden portal.

"The only other thing you need to know at this stage is that aside from the main Houses I've just mentioned, there are also the House of the Ancient Dead, the House of the Illustrious Dead, and the House of the Notorious Dead."

"Sounds like the cemeteries are probably empty."

"Oh no, we have plenty of common dead folk to fill those. We'll encounter these three over our time here together, but you need to know a little about the House of the Ancient Dead in order to fully appreciate what I'm about to show you." Eufame turned to the archway and snapped her fingers.

"Do they have necromancers as well?"

"No, it's staffed by archaeologists. They find and preserve the remains of creatures long dead before we populated this realm. As it happens, a friend of mine works there, and she managed to source something for me."

The white Wolfkin appeared at the doorway, bearing a black chest bound with iron. Jyx estimated the chest to be two feet wide and a foot high. A pair of crossed bones worked in silver adorned the top of the chest and an open padlock hung from the hasp.

"The bones emblem is that of the House of the Ancient Dead," said Eufame.

She lifted the lid and Jyx peered inside. The preserved remains of what looked like a bird lay on a bed of black velvet. Its wings were folded to its sides, with its clawed feet resting on its chest. Its head was bent to one side to accommodate its long beak and pointed skull inside the casket.

"What is it?" asked Jyx.

"It belongs to the pterosaur family, a prehistoric creature that flew in the skies above the swamps and forests that would have originally covered this land. Now, calling the souls of the ancient dead from beyond the veil is trickier than the long dead, but it's balanced out by the fact that animals are easier to recall than humans."

Jyx nodded, unsure as to the purpose of a fossil to the royal coronation proceedings. He ran a finger across the cold skin, wondering who had preserved the creature, and when.

"I said I had a surprise for you, and this is it. I've got a few more menial tasks for you, and once those are done, we'll have a go at raising this pterosaur. It'll be a good introduction to the process, and if it works, you may keep it as a pet. Bastet tells me you've been a little lonely," said Eufame.

Jyx stared up at Eufame, aware his mouth was hanging open. Thoughts of the stolen knowledge hidden in his bedchamber flitted around the edge of his conscious mind, and he pushed the thoughts away. Eufame would never let him raise the pterosaur if she knew what he'd done.

Or maybe she knows and she just doesn't want to let on?

The Wolfkin growled at Eufame. The necromancer rolled her eyes and dipped a slender hand into the bag hanging from the guard's sash. Jyx's heart leapt to see a slim book emerge, its yellowed pages bound in purple leather.

"I'm sure you've re-read your introduction to ritual circles so often you feel your mind might explode through boredom so here is your next text. It's not quite the *Dominantur Umbras* but it will explain the history of our dark science, as well as the basics of necromancy. You'll probably finish it in no time, but I'd like you to study it carefully all the same."

Eufame handed the book to Jyx. He leafed through its pages. His heart sank to see no sigils to practice or incantations to learn, but he fought to keep his disappointment from his face. The *Necromantiae Advenis* was no real substitute for *Impetritae Inceptivus* but it would have to do. At least it wasn't the ritual circles book again.

"Now I've been called back to the palace yet again, and I don't know when I'll be back. That's why I'm giving this to you now. I'd like you to study this in my absence, and we'll see about finishing off the mundane nonsense when I return. That way we can get started on the real work," said Eufame.

She closed the lid of the chest and the Wolfkin retreated into her chambers. Based on the clicking of its claws on the floor, the Wolfkin took the chest into the right hand chamber that led off the atrium. Jyx tried to picture what the room might look like, but all he could see was that vast library of treasure.

Bastet let out a loud miaow and Jyx jumped, suddenly aware of his thoughts. Eufame raised one eyebrow but said nothing. The Wolfkin returned from her chambers, and Eufame clapped her hands.

"Enough for today! Jyx, go and study. Bastet

will keep you company, and I shall see you to-morrow."

Jyx watched the necromancer march along the central aisle. She and the Wolfkin disappeared through the archway leading to the staircase, leaving behind the Wolfkin on guard. Jyx sighed and headed for his own quarters, the *Necromantiae Advenis* loose in his hands. He had a feeling his evening of study would prove to be incredibly dull indeed.

* * * *

The soft thump of a book landing on a stone floor jolted Jyx awake. He looked down to find his hands empty, and the *Necromantiae Advenis* on the floor. He sat forward in the rocking chair and snatched up the book. Looking at the open page, he'd fallen asleep halfway through chapter four. He flicked backwards but nothing looked familiar. Jyx grimaced at the book—in his opinion, books could be hard, or challenging, but they should never be boring.

He hauled himself out of the chair and stretched, wincing as several vertebrae in his spine popped. Something scratched at the back of his mind, like a cat pawing at a doorframe to be allowed inside. Something he'd forgotten was trying to be remembered. Professor Tourney always told him that knowledge was infectious, and once learned, it would try to be used. Jyx shuddered.

"What is it I'm trying to remember, or do?" Jyx's voice sounded hollow in the empty room, and he shrank away from the echo. He frowned. He didn't like his classmates at the Academy, but at least they were people to talk to. Here, he had no one.

Jyx stopped pacing the study and headed into the bedchamber. He picked up a purple velvet pouch from the small dressing table, testing its weight in his hand. The sand inside shifted to accommodate the shape of his palm, and Jyx smiled. He'd created the bag of sleeping sand to practice the geo magick of his Academy days, but now it became a reassuring reminder of what he could do.

A clicking of claws behind him made him jump. Jyx spun around, the pouch slipping from his hand. It landed on the floor in front of Bastet and sent a cloud of sleeping sand into the air. Her nose twitched twice, before she keeled over onto her side.

"Oh no, Bastet? Are you okay? I'm sorry, it was an accident."

Jyx bent down to inspect the cat. Her side rose and fell in time with her gentle snores. Her tail and paws flickered, dreams already occupying her sleeping mind.

"I really hope she doesn't tell Eufame about that." Jyx spoke aloud, more to the mannequins than himself. He shuddered to think what the necromancer general might do if she thought he'd used sleeping sand on purpose—even the fact he'd made some might earn him some sort of punishment.

Jyx walked out into the main Vault. The

doorway leading to the spiral staircase stood unguarded again. Either Eufame had taken the Wolfkin guards with her, or they'd left of their own accord. The tiny hook of fear that had lodged itself in his mind when he arrived wriggled, trying to drag him in the direction of the stairs.

"Don't be silly, Jyx. You can't leave now. You're starting to get to the good stuff, and what would you do if you left?"

He scolded himself, even wagging his finger for good measure. A return to the Academy was out of the question, and Academy dropouts rarely fared well in the Underground City. The educational institutions would break someone with a genuine academic background, and he just wasn't built for manual labour. At least here, at the House of the Long Dead, he had food, shelter, and the possible access to more books than he'd ever have time to read.

Books...

Jyx looked across the Vault towards Eufame's quarters. He thought again of the *Impetritae Inceptivus*, and the forgotten knowledge in his mind burned brighter. The incantations wanted him to learn the words of their siblings; they wanted to be spoken. The illicit sigils begged to be drawn, to have their power unleashed again.

Jyx forced himself to turn away. One trip to the library was enough. He didn't think Eufame knew, but he didn't want to push his luck by chancing another visit. He'd lived on a knife edge since he learned those incantations, constantly working to push the knowledge to the back of his mind until it was time to use it. Another glance at the book would be his undoing.

But the pterosaur...

Jyx smiled. The pterosaur was another matter entirely. All he wanted to do was look at it, to get a sense of its age, and how a resurrection might actually work. Surely Eufame would never have shown him the pterosaur if she didn't want him to be curious. It was only a look. He wasn't going to raise it himself. He wasn't even sure how.

Of course you are...

Knowledge, pieced together from all the texts he'd read, blossomed in his mind. The words learned from the *Impetritae Inceptivus* spun through his thoughts. Jyx forced them aside. At the right time, he'd enjoy being able to demonstrate he possessed such knowledge, but for now, he just wanted to satiate his curiosity.

Jyx headed through the doorway into Eufame's chambers. He ignored the lure of the velvet curtain, and turned right into the other room. More bookshelves lined the walls, although these contained no books of magick or arcane lore. Based on the titles, these were fiction, or works of myth. Jyx recognised one or two novels about a mage who could manipulate time, travelling back and forth to correct the mistakes others had made in their lives. Other titles, this time about an adventurous archaeologist who battled to keep powerful objects out of the wrong hands, caught his eye. The pulp stories were incredibly popular among those rare literate folk in the Underground City.

Vases of varying sizes covered the many tables and chests, each containing beautiful floral
bouquets. On closer inspection, Jyx discovered
the leaves to be the finest velvet, and the stems
to be painted wood. He'd only ever seen a fake floral once before, a ratty old thing his mother had
found in the street, but these were beautiful.

The chest containing the pterosaur lay beside
an overstuffed sofa. Jyx knelt on the floor, glad
Eufame didn't entirely disapprove of rugs, and
ran his hands over the metal bindings. He drew
a small sigil in the air with the third finger of
his left hand, leaving behind a faint trace of pale
blue. The sigil faded, and Jyx smiled. As far as he
could tell, Eufame hadn't placed any protective
seals on the chest. Even the padlock hung open.

Jyx removed the lock and lifted the lid. The
pterosaur lay inside, its wings folded and its
head to one side. It suddenly looked fragile, and
the weight of its age pressed against Jyx's sense
of adventure. He reached out a trembling hand
to stroke the tattered remains of its wing. The
skin, halfway between leather and stone, was
cool to the touch, but Jyx sensed an underly-
ing electricity. An image floated before his mind's
eye, a memory of clean air and space, of blue sky
and freedom.

"I bet you'd love to fly again, wouldn't you?"

Jyx ran his finger along the creature's skull,
marvelling that the memory was not of the pterosaur in flight, but rather the world seen through
its eyes. Jyx delighted in the sensation of weight-
lessness, of riding the air currents far above the

ground, dipping and swooping, master of the horizon.

A low hum caught Jyx's attention and snapped him back to the present. His left arm was outstretched, his index finger pressed against the wooden floor at the edge of the rug. A ring, glowing green with power, pulsed in time with Jyx's heartbeat. His finger rested at the edge of the ring. Jyx gulped, recognising the ring as the Circle of Ani Pe Khamun—just one of many resurrection circles he could have drawn.

Jyx thought of the knowledge he'd been trying to forget. The incantation sprang to his lips, coiling on his tongue like a cobra waiting to strike. The words mirrored the symbols at the edge of the circle, ready to call forth the spirit of the dead. A second incantation, designed to turn sustenance from the ether into sustenance for the physical body, lurked at the back of his throat.

"I could really do this," he said. The electricity in the pterosaur's wing fluttered in response.

"I shouldn't." Jyx wanted to close the chest and leave the room, but as he wracked his brains, he realised he couldn't remember the incantation to close a circle. He couldn't leave it glowing on the floor like that. Eufame would know what he'd done, and even though he'd drawn it by accident, it didn't change the fact he shouldn't even be in her quarters at all.

Jyx tried drawing over the circle backwards, convinced he'd once read that such a process would erase a circle. Instead, the ring glowed brighter as it earthed itself. Jyx groaned—the only way he could dispel the circle would be to actually use it. He reached into the chest and scooped up the pterosaur, cradling it in his arms as though it were a delicate newborn. *In a way, it is.* Eufame would be furious but hopefully a successful resurrection, on his own, would negate any anger she might feel.

"I don't think I should be doing this but I know how to do it, so everything should be fine. You'll be alive again soon, but I think I'll set you free. The world's changed a bit since you were around, but nothing's going to trouble a pterosaur," said Jyx. The pterosaur said nothing in reply.

He placed the pterosaur on the triangle inside the circle, and held his hands over the glowing ring. The incantations swirled and eddied in delight, readying themselves to be spoken aloud. The air grew thick with magickal intent, and Jyx took a deep breath. His nerves sang a song of terror and exhilaration.

"Oh great ones, masters of eternity and guardians of the dark places..." Jyx spoke the words aloud, fighting to suppress the tremor in his voice. The first incantation announced his intention, and altered his consciousness to see beyond the Veil. Shooting stars crossed his vision, and amorphous shapes shifted within the grey mist of the World Beyond. Jyx opened his eyes wide, fighting to see something familiar.

Despite his fear, the second incantation made its way to his lips. This one called out to the spirit of the pterosaur. Jyx spotted its approach, its aura a shining shade of gold, and its lifespan strung out as a field of stars in its wake. Jyx found he could read its story, and saw that the pterosaur died of old age, at peace with the world.

A third incantation, this time in the form of a wordless ballad, issued from Jyx's throat as an undulating stream of music. Fear gripped Jyx as he realised he didn't understand the content of these incantations, and he had no control over the magick he now wielded. He had to trust in the knowledge, and hoped it knew what came next.

The World Beyond faded from view, and Jyx blinked hard. The pterosaur still lay in the middle of the circle, but now its twin, a golden outline of stars, hovered in the still air above it. The fourth and final incantation fell from Jyx's lips, and the soul dropped from the air, melding with the fossil lying on the floor.

Jyx watched as muscle bloomed on the bones, filling the sunken holes and rippling beneath freshly grown skin. The pterosaur twitched, its wings trembling.

"Are you okay?" Jyx knew it was foolish to ask the question, but he felt he needed to say something to fill the silence.

With a screech, the pterosaur hauled itself to its feet, coughing a millennium of dust from its regenerated throat. Jyx couldn't keep the smile from his face. He'd done it.

CHAPTER 9

Jyx looked down at the pterosaur before him. The ritual circle faded, leaving nothing but a light dusting of green powder on the floor. Jyx thought of the ritual broom, and his heart sank. He'd used a ritual circle without cleansing it first. Still, it didn't seem to have affected the pterosaur—it stretched its wings, and flexed its feet.

"Hello, little man. I'm Jyx. Jyximus Faire. I'm your master," said Jyx.

The pterosaur screeched, swinging its head back and forth as if searching for the source of the sound. It scuttled backwards, its claws skittering across the floor.

"It's okay, you don't have to be frightened," said Jyx. He reached out towards the pterosaur but it screeched again, a shriek full of fear and panic. He looked at its reptilian face, and a cold fist of dread punched him in the stomach.

The pterosaur's head snapped from side to side, still hunting for the threat, its dead eyes staring but seeing nothing. It was blind. Jyx's thoughts skipped out of the room towards the cabinet of vials and potions, particularly the *Aperuit oculos* salve. He slapped his hand across his mouth.

"I forgot to anoint the eyes." Jyx forced the words between gritted teeth.

The pterosaur tore at the air with its wings and heaved itself off the floor. It flapped to one side, the joints in its left wing seizing solid. It crashed into the table, and a tall vase of glass lace toppled over. The vase exploded against the floor in a cloud of shards, spilling its fake floral bouquet. Glass blooms lurked among the velvet blossoms, adding their coloured fragments to the powder on the floor.

"No, it's okay, you don't have to panic!" Jyx pleaded with the pterosaur as it worked the kink out of its wing and lurched across the room. It slammed into another table, sending yet another vase flying, which cracked apart into hundreds of porcelain slices.

"No!"

Jyx dived across the room, his fingers missing the pterosaur by a hair's breadth. It howled, a prehistoric sound never before heard by man. With a mighty flap of its wings, it launched itself through the archway. The tip of its wing caught a third vase on the plinth beside the door. Jyx threw himself to the floor and caught the vase before it made contact. He shoved it back onto the plinth before plunging through the archway in pursuit of the pterosaur.

The living fossil made a beeline for the doorway leading back to the main Vault. It let out a series of piercing screams, and Jyx made another grab for its leathery body. The Wolfkin had surely heard the noise, and they would soon be striding through the Vault. The Wolfkin would waste no time in destroying the pterosaur before destroying Jyx too. He caught himself before he could unleash a volley of contemptuous curses, aimed mostly at his own stupidity.

The pterosaur dipped and swooped across the Vault, its claws catching at the mummies on the slabs. Its blind gaze raked across the blank walls, its tongue trying to taste freedom in the cold air. Jyx shouted a warning but the pterosaur failed to pull up in time; it smashed into a table of alchemical apparatus, demolishing the set-up in seconds. Shattered glass covered the floor, and the mixing of the chemicals released noxious fumes. They hung in a dark mist above the stone slabs.

Jyx vaulted over a slab, apologising to its inhabitant. He rifled through his memory, hoping he'd learned some kind of incantation to protect property from damage. Nothing sprang to mind, and he dived to the floor to catch a mummy before it fell from its slab. The ancient king was heavier than Jyx expected, and they landed together in a twisted heap.

"Stop it! Stop destroying everything!"

Jyx threw off the mummy's cadaverous embrace and leapt to his feet. The pterosaur wheeled and flew alongside the wall, its wings brushing the cold stone. It crashed headfirst into the main experimental table, sending flasks and braziers to the floor. Jyx howled, watching the destruction play out. The pterosaur, startled by the noise, flew upwards. It scraped over the gallery rail and smashed into a glass-fronted cabinet of potions.

The pterosaur fell backwards, away from the gallery. It landed on a mummy's stomach with a soft thump. Jyx ran the length of the Vault, his mouth hanging open and tears streaming from his eyes. He reached the pterosaur to find it wasn't dead, simply stunned from the impact.

He scooped up its body and made his way between the slabs to his own quarters. He hurried into his bedchamber, where Bastet still sprawled on the floor, snoring quietly. Jyx put the pterosaur into the empty sarcophagus and scooped a handful of sleeping sand from the floor beside the cat. He sprinkled it over the pterosaur, and its laboured breathing slowed and grew calm.

Jyx stood up and pushed his hands through his hair. He bent to inspect Bastet, but wakefulness would be a long way off for her yet. Perhaps he would have time to clean things up before Eufame got back. He would need to think of an exceptional reason why the pterosaur was missing, but maybe things would be all right.

Jyx walked back into the main Vault. His mouth dropped open as he surveyed the scene. Broken glass littered the floor, and the tables holding the shattered alchemical apparatus smoked under the weight of their chemical burdens. A necromantical residue smeared the walls and most of the surfaces, tracing the pterosaur's destructive path. Jyx didn't even dare return to

Eufame's chambers to check on the breakages in there.

A slow, heavy tread on the spiral staircase turned Jyx's blood to ice water. He stared around at the immense damage. The Wolfkin would punish him for sure. They were too loyal to Eufame not to—and there was nothing he could do to change their loyalties. Unless...

Jyx ran the length of the Vault and crouched in the shadow beside the archway. The descending Wolfkin grunted with each step, and Jyx fancied he could already feel its hot breath on the back of his neck. He steeled himself, and held out his trembling hands. He stared at the patch of stone floor immediately inside the doorway, and visualised a glowing red net of energy.

"*Misit hoc rete, misit fortis, capere umbra, eam mea,*" whispered Jyx. The scarlet strands of power pulsed as they settled across the stones. The net faded, but Jyx heard it hum as it earthed itself. If he squinted, he could see its faint outline. He pushed himself as flat against the wall as he could, as if he wanted to become part of the stones themselves.

The Wolfkin reached the bottom of the stairs and stepped through the archway. Jyx recognised its sleek white fur and smooth muscles. Eufame didn't refer to them by name, or even their specific function, but the white one seemed to most frequently shadow the necromancer general in the Vault. Where that Wolfkin was, Eufame was sure to follow.

Jyx reached out to withdraw the enchantment but the net flared into life, sending crimson sparks skittering into the air. The Wolfkin's head whipped around and its eyes focused on Jyx. Its snarl was cut short as the net became a trap, snapping closed around its shadow.

The fire in the Wolfkin's eyes dulled to a glimmer, and the anger melted from its face. It stumbled backwards and slid down the wall. Its head lolled to one side, gentle snores emanating from the once-fierce head. Jyx stared down at the docile guard, torn between amazement, pride, and fear.

"I've done it... I actually did it. I've taken over a shadow."

Jyx pulled himself to his feet, and peered down at the Wolfkin. Beside it, a Wolfkin-sized shadow swelled to occupy the guard's standing position, its outline tinged with red fire. It flickered before Jyx, but he got the distinct impression it was looking at him. The faint scent of burnt fur hung in the air.

"Hang on, if I can bend a Wolfkin to my will..."

Jyx turned around and looked the length of the Vault. Row upon row of mummies, potential able-bodied assistants, lay before him. His mother had always told him that many hands made light work—surely this many pairs of hands would make the work almost non-existent. He had to try.

"Okay, you. I don't know what your name is, but I know how strong your kind is. You might break free of my net, for all I know, but for now, you do what I tell you. Do you understand?"

The shadow made a movement Jyx took to be a nod. He nodded in reply, and strode off through the Vault. He paused when he reached the central cross point of the aisles, and looked towards Eufame's chambers. Part of him told him to double check his incantations. He shook his head to dispel the doubts. He turned to address the shadow, glad of someone to talk to.

"I know I should check the incantations but I really don't have time. Miss Delsenza could be back at any time, and I don't know how long it's going to take to raise a whole room of mummies."

Jyx paused to count them. He didn't think he would need all of them—possibly only half. Maybe even just ten of them would do. They could be sweeping up the broken glass while he laid protective enchantments on the spilled chemicals to prevent them doing any more damage. If they were quick enough, he could even form new glass from the shards to re-glaze the cabinets in the gallery. He couldn't rescue the enchantments from the broken bottles, but that couldn't be helped. He'd never seen Eufame use them so far; perhaps she kept them more for show than for practical use.

"I think it'll be fine. After all, everything worked on the pterosaur; it only went wrong because it couldn't see, so it panicked. I've anointed their eyes so they'll be able to see. Besides, look how easy it was to ensnare you."

Jyx pinched himself, unable to believe that he was freely talking to a shadow—and a shadow of a Wolfkin, at that. If only Dean Whittaker could see him now! Apprentice to the necromancer general, and master of a shadow—he would have to make the wall of alumni now.

Jyx fetched the ritual broom from its perch over the doorway to Eufame's quarters, and handed it to the shadow. Jyx paced the floor around the slabs, careful to draw the correct sigils at the correct points of the circle. He frowned that he couldn't draw an exact circle, due to the arrangement of the slabs and the dimensions of the Vault, but he was sure it wouldn't matter. As long as the circle was complete and the sigils were in place, it should be fine. The shadow followed him, sweeping the broom from side to side. Jyx couldn't hear it speaking the words of banishment, but he felt them resonating all the same.

He returned to his starting point, and the circle manifested in a blast of green energy. Jyx heaved a sigh of relief and turned to the shadow. He took back the ritual broom and returned it to its place above the door.

"You see? That was what I did with the pterosaur, but I need you to go and keep watch. Do not let anyone in, you understand?"

The shadow gave another imperceptible nod and drifted towards the doorway. Jyx made his way to the centre of the circle, or as close as he could get to it, and closed his eyes. A magickal current thrummed in the air, like a sustained bass note, and Jyx took a deep breath.

"Oh great ones, masters of eternity and guardians of the dark places…"

His consciousness slipped sideways with

every beat of the incantation, and he fought the urge of his spirit to lurch to the west. His mind's eye snapped open, and the grey mists of the World Beyond filled his vision. The shades of those who had gone before hovered on the edge of his perception.

A second incantation sprang to his lips. He danced along a sparkling silver cord, flitting from shade to shade in the World Beyond. He invited the souls of the departed royalty to return, to find their old bodies and to live again. The souls massed as shining figures of gold and silver, starlight dancing in their eyes. Even in the World Beyond, Jyx heaved a sigh of relief. They could see.

The third incantation poured out of his throat. He still didn't know what the notes signified, or what power they held over the dead, but they'd worked on the pterosaur, and now they'd work on the mummies. The figures loomed closer, the starlight seeming brighter and more intense, as the World Beyond faded from view.

Jyx opened his eyes to see a series of silver shadows drifting between the slabs. The shades peered down at the mummies, ignoring the ones they didn't recognise, and clambering up onto the slab when they found themselves. Sweat snaked down Jyx's back, and he realised he hadn't spoken the final incantation yet. They were getting ahead of him.

He allowed his lips to form the fourth and final incantation. Power coursed through him, and out of him, charging the air with palpable energy. The faint tang of ozone filled the room.

The souls lay down to meld with the mummies on the slabs, disappearing into the desiccated bodies within seconds. Their collective gasps for air tore apart the silence of the Vault, and Jyx's ears were filled with the dry, hitching chokes of bodies seeking to breathe.

CHAPTER 10

Queen Neferpenthe sat up, coughing up clouds of ancient dust. Jyx forced himself to uproot his feet from the floor. He didn't want to move too quickly and risk panicking the mummy, but he didn't have time on his side. He still expected to hear Eufame descending the stairs, and his thoughts flew to the skeleton embedded in the marble floor upstairs.

"Hello?"

She turned her head to face him, her joints whining in protest. She pried her eyelids open with gnarled fingers, and stared at him with hollow eye sockets. Sparks fizzed in the depths of her skull. The weight of her gaze reminded him of Dean Whittaker. Jyx forced down a gulp.

"Can you see me?" Jyx hoped the mummy would have a magical ability to speak his language, but gestured to himself in case she didn't.

The mummy bared her sharp yellow teeth and hissed. Jyx let out a tiny gasp, and looked at the Wolfkin shadow, searching its depths for answers. It shrugged in reply, and drifted through the Vault, pausing behind Jyx. His own shadow shrank away from contact with the red-ringed silhouette.

Other mummies sat up in the lower half of the Vault, and pried open their eyes. Some of them let out cries of despair or confusion. The cold air of the Vault smelled of age and stale dust, the scent of arrested decay hanging heavy around him. The last shreds of hope fluttered in his heart, and Jyx made his way between the slabs. His skin crawled to feel the stares of so many empty eye sockets.

"I know you can all see me, and I've raised you a bit earlier than planned to help me out," said Jyx. His gaze flittered from slab to slab, but he couldn't see their shadows.

Do the dead even have shadows?

Queen Neferpenthe swung her legs over the side of the slab, and her feet slapped onto the stone floor. She pushed herself upright and swayed. The moonstone in her diadem glinted in the flickering light from the braziers. She steadied herself against the slab, but her head rolled from side to side. She reminded Jyx of the drunkards he'd encountered in the Underground City. Perhaps they weren't drunkards; perhaps they were escapees from the graveyards. Jyx forced the thought from his mind.

"Good, you're keen, I'm glad, but—"

The mummy planted one foot in front of her and dragged the other foot level. Triumph crossed her pinched features. With a cry of delight, she propelled herself forward another step. She released her grip on the slab and shuffled across the aisle, her joints creaking and protesting with every jerky movement. She headed for the smoking remains of the alchemical table along the western wall.

"No, it's okay, I was going to tidy that—"

She hooked her fingers under the edge of the table and heaved upwards. Both the table and the mummy's muscles groaned with the effort, and the last of the apparatus toppled to the floor with a crash. Unnamed chemicals mixed in the cracks between the flagstones, releasing coloured fumes with a hiss. Queen Neferpenthe released her hold on the table, still too weak to overturn it. She looked down at the broken flasks and dented braziers and let out a victorious cry.

The rebellion rippled through the mummies, and withered legs swung from the slabs in the lower half of the Vault. Jyx raked his hands through his hair, searching the floor for signs of shadows. At least then he could control them. He saw none—even the mummies nearest the braziers cast no shadows.

"Would you please just help me?"

The mummies all turned to face Jyx. Silence descended in the Vault, broken only by the rasping breathing of the assembled royalty. Jyx scanned their empty faces, searching for a shred of humanity. He saw nothing but vacant death. Despair was forced aside as panic seized him by the throat and he fought to breathe.

Queen Neferpenthe held up her arms, her hands trembling under the weight of the withered muscle. She opened her mouth and hacked up another lungful of dust. Jyx recognised the pose from his readings and leapt forward to stop her mid-incantation. Before he could reach her, she uttered three long, guttural syllables. Fragments of energy flickered in the ether, disappearing into the waiting mouths of the mummies.

"Why won't you just do what I'm asking?"

Jyx screamed at the mummies, anger and fear tussling for control over his nerves. He thought of the *Impetritae Inceptivus* with fury. They weren't just initial incantations—the book contained serious magick, and it should have contained a warning. The *Dominantur Umbras* did. Besides, what kind of magician kept books with pages that were stuck together? There could be all manner of useful or important information on those pages.

A nagging hook of doubt buried itself in the back of Jyx's mind. Before he could consider it further, the mummies roared in unison, and scattered. Emboldened by Queen Neferpenthe's rebellion and nourished by the ether, they lurched between the slabs. Two of the younger royals pushed over a slab, crowing about their achievement as the marble hit the floor with a crash. Queen Neferpenthe led three mummies up the spiral staircase to the gallery, where they set about smashing the remaining cabinets and destroying their contents. Hundreds of enchantments flickered around the room, hanging in the air like persistent fireflies.

Jyx ran to the end of the Vault. Several pairs of paws pounded down the stairs, the shadows of more Wolfkin looming large against the stone wall. The Wolfkin by the doorway stirred, and the shadow at Jyx's shoulder drifted towards it.

"No! I haven't released you! I need your help to control these mummies!" Jyx reached out his hands, both in terror and supplication. The shadow was the only element of control he still had, and he wasn't keen to let it go.

The Wolfkin's shadow sank to the floor and reattached itself to the Wolfkin's hind paws. The guard's eyes snapped open, and the Wolfkin leapt to its feet. It bared its teeth in a vicious snarl, and loomed over Jyx. Hot canine breath licked at his face, and its left paw landed on his shoulder. Claws gripped his skin through his robe, and Jyx yelped as the talons dug into the thin flesh over his shoulder blade.

Two more Wolfkin appeared in the doorway behind the monster before him. They surveyed the devastation in the Vault, taking in the broken apparatus, the shattered cabinets and the overturned slabs. Jyx turned to see Queen Neferpenthe bent over one of the unraised mummies. He shouted a warning, but the Wolfkin cuffed him around the head with its other paw. Stars exploded across Jyx's vision, and he reeled from the impact. The Wolfkin dug in its claws further, holding him firm.

The newly arrived Wolfkin barked to each

other. The black Wolfkin turned and ran back up the stairs. The tawny Wolfkin barged into the Vault, shoving Jyx aside with a massive shoulder, and caught a mummy by the scruff of his neck. Jyx recognised him as Prince Amen-Atep, one of the current ruler's great-great-great-great uncles. The Wolfkin holding Jyx lifted him off his feet, and Jyx howled from the pain. Blood ran down his back inside his robe, the fabric clinging to the sticky fluid.

The mummies paused mid-destruction. Every pair of eyes turned his way, and ancient nostrils caught his scent. Jyx whimpered in the Wolfkin's grasp, unable to twist around or free himself.

"Please...let me go..."

The Wolfkin growled at him, but lowered him to the floor. It kept its eyes on the watching mummies and retracted its claws. Jyx collapsed to his knees, clutching his bleeding shoulder. He'd never studied the various healing arts, always considering them to be beneath him. Now, injured and in pain, he realised that such talents could have a real purpose.

The tawny Wolfkin yelped, a thin, high noise that pierced the air of the Vault. Jyx looked up to see it drop the mummy, and clutch its paw to its chest. The mummy whirled and hissed at the Wolfkin, baring his bloodied teeth. He pounced on the guard, knocking it backwards. The white Wolfkin leapt forward to catch its kin, and the dead prince howled. The other mummies stood frozen in the Vault, twitching as they looked between the battle and the door.

Jyx struggled to his feet, still clutching his shoulder. His robes were now sodden and stuck to the wound. He tried to visualise the net he would need to capture the two shadows of the white and tawny Wolfkin, but Prince Amen-Atep rallied himself. He sprang forward, knocking the tawny Wolfkin into the arms of the white Wolfkin. All three hit the floor with a crash, and the mummy pounded the chest of the tawny Wolfkin with his fists. Another mummy shuffled across the aisle, this one an ancient princess. She aimed a hefty kick at the ribs of the white Wolfkin; its once threatening barks and growls turned to pathetic whimpers.

Jyx couldn't see their shadows. He looked at the mummies, still gathered in the Vault, staring at him. He couldn't rely on the Wolfkin for help, and the mummies wouldn't obey him. There was only one thing left to do.

Jyx hurled himself through the doorway and scrabbled up the stairs. Half running, half pulling himself upwards with his good arm, he was out of sight of the Vault when he heard the first mummies reach the stairwell. They groaned with exertion, and snapped at each other as they fought to swarm up the spiral stairs.

* * * *

Jyx spilled out of the archway and into the main vestibule of the house. A small throng of young men in dark brown habits stood near the grand staircase, attended by a Wolfkin clad in leather armour. Jyx ignored their stares as he scrambled across the hall, panic-stricken and disorientated.

An angry screech burst forth from the archway, followed by a hissing ball of fur. Bastet streaked past him and shot out of the front doors of the House. A stab of guilt attacked Jyx's stomach as he realised he'd forgotten all about her. Having seen how the mummies attacked the Wolfkin, little Bastet was better off out of the Vault.

Two mummies lunged into the vestibule, outstretched fingers bent into vicious hooks. Jyx dodged their reach and pelted towards the front door. The two Wolfkin that guarded the entrance lowered their ceremonial pikes and growled. Jyx stared at them, a plea burning in his eyes.

Please let me past, please let me past.

He threw himself left then right to avoid the pikes, and he passed the Wolfkin without a glance from either of them. They snarled at the following mummy horde. Jyx allowed himself to look over his shoulder, and at least ten of the long-dead royals had made it into the hall. The young men in habits fled screaming up the stairs, their cries drawing the attention of the mummies. A handful of the dead royals pursued the novices upwards, stumbling and scrambling up the wide staircase.

Jyx turned away and raced out of the doors. A squad of Wolfkin charged towards him, drawn by the sounds of the fracas inside. The lead Wolfkin picked him up by the shoulder and lifted him aside in one smooth movement. Jyx screamed in pain, the claws digging into the fresh wounds left by the last Wolfkin to grip his shoulder. The

Wolfkin dropped him and Jyx rolled across the threshold. A trail of blood traced his route along the marble floor.

The squad disappeared into the gloom of the house. Screeching and growling fought each other for supremacy before the large entrance doors swung closed with a resounding crash. Jyx sank to his knees on the steps, aware that another crowd of Eufame's admirers stood watching across the courtyard. They took in the sight of his injuries, and they backed away until they met the wall.

Bastet miaowed. Jyx looked up and saw her perched on top of a pedestal near the door. She wound herself around the statue's feet, glaring at Jyx as she did so.

"I'm so sorry, Bastet. I didn't mean to use the sleeping sand, and I thought you'd be safe in my chamber."

She miaowed again, her golden eyes full of reproach. Jyx hung his head. *She knows I forgot about her. I am a horrible person.*

"Miss Delsenza's probably going to embed me in the floor, isn't she?"

Bastet flicked her tail in reply. Jyx stared at the ground. Only two weeks ago, his biggest worry had been ensuring no one found out about his nocturnal visits to the library. Now he had a horde of dead royals rampaging around inside one of the city's oldest institutions—and it was all *his* fault. Expulsion from the Academy would have been better than this.

The tall doors swung open. Jyx looked up,

and peered into the gloom. He expected to see mummies strewn across the floor as victorious Wolfkin stood over them, nursing their war wounds. Instead, a horde of mummies swarmed out of the front door, leaving dark heaps on the floor inside the House—dark, broken heaps of muscle and fur. Jyx gulped and looked away, unwilling to see the destruction wrought inside.

Several mummies broke away from the main group and lumbered across the courtyard towards Eufame's would-be suitors. The old men stood rooted to the spot, staring wide-eyed at the advancing royals.

"Run, you idiots!" Jyx shouted at them, ignoring the fire in his shoulder to make wild "leave now" gestures with his arms. The mummies fell upon the small group, knocking the suitors to the ground. Screams and pleas for mercy overwhelmed the sounds of tearing and crunching.

The rest of the pack turned their attention towards Jyx. He looked across the courtyard but a small detachment of resurrected princes blocked his route to the exit. Another group blocked the doors to the house. There was nowhere to go, except through the mummies.

The scent of the yellowed pages in the *Impetritae Inceptivus* filled his nostrils, and the words sprang unbidden to Jyx's lips. He threw back his head and yelled "*Extollat me, exalta me altum, liberabis me, ut volet!*" A gust of wind gathered behind him and forced him upwards. His feet left the ground and he felt himself launched towards the pedestal. Jyx caught the cold stone in his outstretched hands and he scrabbled onto the slab. He clung to the plinth beside Bastet. He was torn between elation at using his first wind magick incantation, and terror at the sight of so many mummies.

"I don't understand it, Bastet. I'm sure I didn't raise that many."

Bastet miaowed and looked down into the courtyard. Jyx followed her golden gaze to where Queen Neferpenthe stood in the doorway. Another battalion of mummies gathered behind her, and Jyx's heart plummeted when he saw Wolfkin among her death squad.

"She did it? She raised the others, and the dead Wolfkin? Why didn't anyone tell me she was a necromancer too?"

Bastet miaowed again and gave an almost imperceptible shake of her head. Jyx stared down at the queen. Nourished by blood as well as ether, her body had filled out and fewer wrinkles folded her ancient skin. Red sparks fizzed in the depths of her eye sockets, and her mouth curved into a rictus grin.

The thundering sound of hooves on stone and the panicked whinny of horses poured into the courtyard. Eufame strode through the arch, flanked by her personal guard. Her cold eyes burned with fierce rage, and Jyx could feel the sharp spikes of her aura all the way across the yard.

"What in the name of the Old and Great Ones is going on here?"

Eufame's voice boomed across the courtyard.

The notes of both fury and menace were enough to stop the mummies in their tracks. Those nearest the arch cowered backwards, away from the familiar figure of the necromancer general. Two of the mummies hunched over the remains of the suitors paused in their feeding frenzy to note the new arrival. Jyx glanced at Neferpenthe; the mummy queen scowled at Eufame.

Bastet let out a long howl, and Eufame looked up to the pedestal. Her expression softened for a fraction of a second when she recognised the cat. Her face hardened when her gaze alighted on Jyx.

"You. This was your doing."

Eufame gave a flick of her wrist and Jyx tumbled from the pedestal. He landed on the ground with a thump, the air forced out of his body. His shoulder protested, and a loud whine filled in the air. It was only when the shock of the impact faded that Jyx realised the whining came from him. He looked across the courtyard, and Eufame gazed back. Disappointment and fury chased each other across her sharp features.

"I'm sorry, it was an accident—"

"I'll deal with you later."

Eufame rolled back the draped sleeves of her robe to reveal thin white arms covered in dark red designs. They resembled the pictographic writing Jyx had seen inside the house, and he guessed they were arcane tattoos, although they bore an uncanny resemblance to dried blood. She pointed at the mummies nearest to her. They halted their slow creep towards her, and froze several feet away.

The Wolfkin guard accompanying Eufame spread out to take up their positions around her. She barked several words in a guttural language. The raised Wolfkin among Queen Neferpenthe's squad stepped aside, and marched down the steps. They lined up against the outer wall of the house. The mummy queen shrieked and barked out a frenzy of her own, but the Wolfkin dropped their weapons and put their paws behind their heads. One of Eufame's guard broke away to gather their weapons. The Wolfkin stood between its raised kin and Queen Neferpenthe, a low growl rumbling in its throat.

Jyx scrambled to his feet and hobbled across the courtyard. Eufame ignored him as he slipped past. The Wolfkin behind her prevented an escape from the house, but at least he'd be safer behind Eufame than in front of her. Safe for now, at least.

Eufame roared and green fire sprang in a circle around the perimeter of the courtyard. The mummies closest to it shrieked and fell back. Jyx recognised the symbols around the circle, although they were inverted from those he'd drawn. Only two were completely different—and came from the *Book of Banishment*.

"You're going to banish them?"

"You leave me no choice, Jyx."

Eufame chanted the first incantation. The words sliced through the air like darts made of ice, leaving visible trails of cold. Queen Neferpenthe, standing just outside the circle, waved her hands and shrieked a counter spell. The flames flickered, but held. Eufame narrowed her eyes and repeated the incantation with a little more force. Queen Neferpenthe snapped her fingers and the mummies nearest Eufame broke their trance and lurched forward.

Three of the Wolfkin took up positions in front of the necromancer general. Immense blades dangled from sheaths attached to their belts, and they wielded vicious maces. Jyx ducked around Eufame and drew a sigil in the dust on the marble paving. A tiny whirlwind, no more than a foot high, spun through the dust, sending it flying upwards and into the empty eye sockets of the advancing mummies. They stopped, clawing at their faces, the enchanted dust interfering with their necromantic sight. The mummies fell to the ground, their goal of reaching Eufame forgotten.

"Nicely done, Jyx. But ultimately pointless," said Eufame.

"Why? I thought you wouldn't want the bodies destroyed," replied Jyx.

"Are you really as stupid as you look? These souls have been tainted through blood. I cannot separate them from their bodies, and then perform the ritual again, albeit correctly." Her scornful tone slashed Jyx's pride. "No, these creatures must be destroyed!"

Eufame unleashed another incantation. A whirlwind, much larger than that created by Jyx, tore around the circle. Spectral hands of tempestuous air clawed at the mummies. Souls were ripped free from ancient bodies, whipped away within the whirlwind to spiral out of sight. The lifeless corpses swayed where they stood before collapsing into heaps of desiccated flesh and papery skin.

Queen Neferpenthe raised her arms and threw her head back, her withered vocal cords forming jagged syllables of raw power. The mummies around the circle surged forward, spurred on by their leader. Eufame growled and a ripple of energy danced around the sigils. The mummies collided with a wall of banishment. Arms of green magick reached out of the wall, tearing the souls free from any mummies found to be within their grasp.

"Come on, 'Penthe! Send me some more of your cronies!" Eufame screamed across the courtyard. Jyx sneaked a look at the necromancer general. Determination set her face in a mask of cold focus. He bit his lip to see a droplet of blood at her nostril.

Queen Neferpenthe lowered her arms and twisted her mouth into a parody of a pout. Only those mummies behind her remained. The rest of her impromptu army lay scattered around the courtyard, both inside and outside Eufame's circle.

"What is she going to do?" asked Jyx.

"There is really only one thing she can do. Give up."

"Is that likely?"

"No."

Eufame barked a command and the green circle of flames subsided. The lifeless bodies in the courtyard suddenly looked fragile and pitiful. If he hadn't seen them clash with the Wolfkin, he'd never have believed them capable of such violence.

"What are you doing?" Jyx trotted after Eufame as she stalked across the courtyard, her loyal guard in tow. Green energy glowed from within her tattoos, and snaked down her forearms. It clustered in her open hands, cupped as if to carry water. Queen Neferpenthe paced back and forward, her eye sockets fixed on the growing mass of energy in Eufame's hands. The necromancer general pulled at the mass, sculpting it and drawing it into new shapes. Eufame fashioned the energy into a glowing green scythe.

The remnants of Queen Neferpenthe's personal guard surged past their leader. Eufame swung the scythe once, and the blade screamed as it sliced through the air. It slid through the approaching mummies, and their lifeless corpses fell to their knees. Their souls remained standing for a moment, sliced in half, before they winked out of existence. The bodies swayed in front of Eufame before they stumbled backwards, landing with a series of wet thumps on the marble steps.

Jyx looked at the dead royals strewn around the courtyard. Blood smeared their mouths and stained their ancient skin. Jyx didn't need Eufame's advanced powers of perception to know their souls would carry the Blood Taint. *She must have banished them to the Nether World, and there's no coming back from there.*

Queen Neferpenthe screamed. She pried the moonstone from her diadem and tucked it into the palm of one hand. She brought her hands together with a mighty crash. The moonstone exploded in a shower of white sparks, and the shockwave threw Eufame and Jyx backwards. Jyx landed on a broken mummy, and his shoulder wound sent spikes of pain coursing through him. He cried out, and rolled to the side. The movement forced a final puff of air out of the mummy's lungs. A foetid smell hung in the air.

"Is that all you have, 'Penthe?"

Jyx looked up. Eufame struggled to regain her footing, the green scythe of energy now pulsing in her hand. Queen Neferpenthe breathed on the ball of white energy in her hands, turning the energy an inky shade of black. She stretched it and moulded it between her fingers as Eufame scrambled to her feet. Neferpenthe formed the black energy into a crackling labrys. She swung it backward in a neat arc, and grunted as she heaved it forward over her head.

The blade of the labrys connected with the staff of Eufame's scythe as Eufame brought it up in defence. Neferpenthe screeched and threw herself forward, driving Eufame back two steps, the necromancer's muscles taut as she fought to keep the labrys at bay.

Jyx pushed himself to his feet. The setting sun threw long shadows across the courtyard. While the other mummies still cast none, Queen Neferpenthe's shadow stretched out for several feet behind her, crackling with the same energy visible in her labrys. Jyx visualised a sparkling red net, and drew back his hands as he prepared to cast it across the mummy's new shadow.

Queen Neferpenthe squealed and hauled the labrys away from Eufame. The necromancer general stumbled, pulled off balance by the mummy's movement. Neferpenthe swung the labrys again, preparing to take a swing at Jyx.

Jyx cast his net but his aim went wide. Eufame took advantage of the diversion. With one fluid movement, she heaved the scythe in a ragged arc, and sliced the blade through Neferpenthe.

Queen Neferpenthe swayed on her feet. Her hands flew to her throat and she dropped the labrys. The axe exploded in a frenzy of black shards when it hit the ground. Eufame jabbed at her with the scythe, and Queen Neferpenthe fell backwards. A shade of her former self remained standing, her soul manifest before them. Eufame barked a short incantation, and drove the scythe through the centre of the shade. Both the soul and the scythe disappeared in a flash of green.

"That bitch never did know when to quit," said Eufame. Blood trickled from both nostrils, and silver streaked her hair. Tiny wrinkles clustered at the outer edges of her eyes, eyes now dull with exertion.

"I'm so sorry, I really am, I—"

"Enough."

Eufame stood up and her Wolfkin guard trotted over. They flanked her, cutting Jyx off from his mentor. Jyx wanted to tell her his side, but the Wolfkin rushed her into the House of the Long Dead, and out of sight.

CHAPTER 11

"My Vault...my wonderful Vault..."

Jyx found Eufame in the Vault, standing just inside the door. She gazed the length of the chamber, her jaw slack. Jyx noticed a film of moisture in her eyes and looked away. A combination of remorse and shame burned in his chest, fanned by the knowledge that everything was his fault. The flame burned brighter when he thought of his mother's inevitable disappointment. Eufame swept along the central aisle, her robes trailing in pools of smoking alchemical compounds. Bastet followed, picking her way through the debris on her velvet paws. Eufame disappeared through the archway in the wall to inspect the damage in her chambers.

Jyx stood by the Vault's entrance. One of Eufame's personal guard stood uncomfortably close behind him. Jyx stared at the ceiling, unable to bring himself to look at the destruction. Over-turned marble slabs lay all around the room, and traces of gold glittered among the wreckage of the alchemy tables. Two of the raised Wolfkin swept up the broken glass from the display cabinets in the gallery, while another moved counter-clock-wise, sprinkling handfuls of dust around the pe-rimeter of the Vault. Only a handful of mummies lay untouched at the far end of the room. A tiny glimmer of relief flickered in Jyx's mind to see Eufame's favourite royal among them.

A heart-rending scream echoed around the Vault, issuing from Eufame's chamber. The depth of sorrow turned the scream white, and it coa-lesced as a mist of sadness that clung to the walls.

"She's going to kill me, isn't she?" asked Jyx, turning to the Wolfkin guard behind him.

The guard growled in reply. Jyx tried to swal-low the hard ball of fear lodged in his throat.

Eufame reappeared in the Vault, her fists clenched tight and her mouth set in a firm line. She stalked up the central aisle towards Jyx. He flinched, caught between Eufame's confron-tational aura and the aggressive stance of the Wolfkin behind him.

Jyx wanted to ask how bad the damage was but he managed only a whimper. The noise sounded small and hollow in the cavernous room.

"You are lucky, Master Faire, that the damage is confined to only one of my chambers. The li-brary remains untouched, as do my other rooms. But you already know of my library, don't you?"

"I...I...yes I do."

"Judging by the stink your aura has left, you favoured the *Impetritae Inceptivus*, didn't you?"

Jyx nodded. Only a handful of magickal practitioners could physically smell auras; he should have known Eufame would be one of them.

"I knew you would head straight for that one. And you omitted the vital clause in the *Resurrectio Totalis* incantation, didn't you?"

Jyx stared at her. "What vital clause?"

"This is the reason why I instructed you not to enter the library without correct supervision or guidance! The vital clause is there to ensure the raised spirits remain pliant and docile."

Jyx thought of the pages, gummed together with old candle wax. His legs buckled and he pitched forward. The Wolfkin grabbed his collar and pulled him upright.

"Yes, Jyx. Some of the pages were stuck together, weren't they? You learned the incantation that you found on the page, but you didn't check to make sure you'd copied out the whole incantation. You absolute fool. I bet you thought you were going to impress me, didn't you?"

Jyx tried to nod but fear, guilt, and anger at his own stupidity kept him paralysed.

"That pterosaur was never a test for you, nor was it a vehicle for you to show off how talented you think you are! It was intended as a learning tool, and now you've left the poor thing blind and confused!" Eufame jabbed a slender finger at Jyx's chest.

"I'm sorry."

"Oh I bet you are but sorry just isn't good

enough. Because of you, I've lost a trove of personal possessions that are utterly irreplaceable. I've lost almost an entire collection of enchantments. My alchemical work will need to be begun from scratch and the new prince's coronation procession has been left in ruins!"

Jyx stared at the floor, willing it to open and swallow him whole. Visions of his mother, so elated at his promotion to necromancer's apprentice, danced before his mind's eye. He saw Dean Whittaker, so stern and disapproving, and the Wolfkin, so angry with humanity for ages-old injustices carried into the new world. He remembered the intoxication of seeing the World Beyond, and his joy at performing shadow magick for the first time. But a spectre hovered at the edge of his inner sight, a spectre clad in the absent colours of infinity, a spectre with the voice of Time itself.

"I had such high hopes for you, Jyx. That's what makes all of this worse than it needs to be. The disappointment. You could have been magnificent. A real force to be reckoned with." Eufame cracked her knuckles. Jyx winced.

"What are you going to do?"

"If it had just been my work, or my things, that had been destroyed, then it would have been a punishment of some sort. Perhaps I would have cast you in amber and had you mounted as some sort of living wall art. Maybe I would have had you added to the Gallery of Sinners that you saw on your way in here. Oh yes, those are not statues. They are petrified former employees."

"The Gallery of Sinners?" Jyx remembered the statues around the walls of the house and his knees threatened to buckle beneath him.

"Oh yes. You committed at least two sins—greed and pride. I'm sure if I thought about it I could come up with more. You couldn't be content to simply wait and be taught at your true pace, could you?"

"It was an accident! I wanted to see what kind of books you had and I don't know, the words just seemed to stick in my brain, and they wanted me to say them! I didn't mean to raise the pterosaur, it just happened!" Jyx clamped his hands over his mouth but the outburst had been said, and hung in the air like a poisonous miasma.

"Knowledge does that, Jyx. It wants to be used. No, more than that—it needs to be used. Now, knowledge in a normal man is bad enough, but magickal knowledge in the hands of one who is not ready...that's just never going to end well for anyone. You may have done this entirely by accident, but that doesn't change the fact that it happened."

The Wolfkin behind Jyx let out a series of short barks. Eufame nodded and clasped her hands together in front of her.

"My esteemed guard here wishes to remind you that as a result of your actions, eight Wolfkin have been lost today. True, a raised Wolfkin can still serve a purpose, as you can see here, since their bodies have always had a different relationship with their souls, but that is still a waste by anybody's reckoning."

Jyx watched the raised Wolfkin bustle around the Vault, performing their set tasks with the sort of clear-minded determination he'd only ever seen in the trolls of the Underground City. Eufame could earn a fortune if she sold them on as household staff.

"Of course, there is a further consideration. Regardless of any injury or damage that you may have caused to me or the Wolfkin, there is the fact that the prince's procession will have to be called off. Incurring the wrath of a necromancer general is nothing compared to the wrath of a petulant and spoiled brat like our would-be king. I'm afraid he will order an execution when he finds out it was you."

Eufame stared at him hard. Jyx saw no trace of sadness in her face. She wasn't afraid of an execution order at all.

"Why does he have to find out?" Jyx heard the whine in his voice and despised himself, but he couldn't help it. He didn't want to die, and he wasn't entirely sure that an execution was a fair punishment for an accident. If Eufame could command Wolfkin, surely she could cover this up.

"I'm going to pretend you didn't say that, Jyx. He will want an execution, and he will want a fate worse than death. Because of the total disregard you have shown to me and my home, as well as your headstrong propensity to disobey orders, not to mention the fact that you left Bastet down here with a mob of bloodthirsty mummies, then I have no option but to condemn you to the Perpetual Death."

Jyx gasped as cold vomit gathered in his stomach, threatening to expel itself upward at the thought of an imminent, and not entirely understood, death. He shuddered in the Wolfkin's grasp, ignoring the insistent pain in his shoulder.

"What's that?"

"I have to kill you, Jyx. Don't worry, I will make it quick and painless as I am not entirely cruel and without mercy. But I will need to resurrect you...and kill you again."

"You can't do that!"

"I can, Jyx. And worst of all—I will."

The Wolfkin took Jyx's collar in one massive paw and lifted him off the ground. The collar bit into his throat and cut short his cries of indignation. Flames of agony burned in his torn shoulder, and Jyx resisted the urge to struggle, knowing every movement made the fire burn harder.

Eufame strode away down the Vault, and swept into her chambers. The Wolfkin followed, holding Jyx aloft as it picked its way through the rubble of broken slabs. The raised Wolfkin paid them no attention at all, too focused on the tasks set by their mistress.

They passed through the vestibule. The curtain screening the library from view hung undisturbed in front of them. Eufame ignored the doorway to her right and instead passed through the left-hand doorway. Jyx had never seen inside the room, and he could only guess at what lay beyond the dark portal. His stomach turned to ice, and threatened to evacuate its contents all over the floor.

A short passage led from the vestibule into a large round chamber. A vast ritual circle was inscribed into the black marble floor in mother-of-pearl, its markings utterly alien to Jyx's eyes. A lofty ceiling sloped upward to the inverted obelisk, which hung from the apex. A low slab stood in the centre of the room, directly below the obelisk. Cages of different sizes hung from the walls. They were empty, although Jyx could only imagine what Eufame normally kept in them. Large alcoves punctured the wall at regular intervals.

Eufame pointed to the slab, and the Wolfkin deposited Jyx in a heap on the cold stone. The guard forced him onto his back, pushed his legs straight and folded his arms across his chest, each hand gripping the opposite biceps. Jyx stared up at the ceiling, the obelisk pointing at him like an accusing finger. *It was you*, it seemed to say. *It was all your fault, and you deserve everything you get.*

Eufame stood on the opposite side of the room, her back to them as she rummaged in an ebony cabinet against the wall. Jyx looked beyond the Wolfkin towards the doorway. He had never seen a Wolfkin run, but they were so bulky and heavy compared to his lithe frame.

If I make a run for it, how far might I get? The Wolfkin outside were ordered to tidy up, not stop me, and there are no guards on the doors now.

Eufame snapped her fingers. Icy claws gripped Jyx's feet, and a wave of frost passed up his legs and into his body. Whatever the frost touched, Jyx found he could no longer feel. He looked down and saw his feet, his toes pointing towards the ceiling, but they felt as though they belonged to someone else. No amount of effort could make his feet move.

"You're not going anywhere, Jyx, so I'd think better of running if I were you. Better to accept your punishment. You'll find it much easier in the World Beyond if you do," said Eufame.

She barked to the Wolfkin. He nodded and left the chamber. Eufame leaned over Jyx and he shuddered as fear made his muscles spasm. Her expression softened slightly as she brushed a lock of black hair from his face.

"Jyx, here in the space on the edge of the world, I feel I should explain. I always knew this would happen. In fact, you could say I counted on it," she said. "The prince would have you hung, drawn and quartered like a common criminal, but you're no criminal, and you're not common."

"I'm so sorry, and I'm so scared."

Jyx's lip wobbled and the tears held in check behind his eyes finally broke free. Salty water blurred his vision and oozed from the corners of his eyes. Eufame wiped the first of the tears away with her cold thumb.

"I know you are, Jyx, but I also know there was no malice behind what you did, and you have served your purpose well."

"My purpose?"

"Do you know why I chose you, Jyx?"

"Because I was about to be expelled?"

"That made it easier, but it wasn't the reason. No, the real reason was that you overstretch yourself. You run when you should be learning to walk. I was counting on you doing the same thing here. Every time I held you back, I knew you would fight to move forward."

"You set this all up?"

"Indeed I did, Jyx. The prince has been making noises about replacing me for some time. I represent the old regime of his forebears, and he wants an entirely new set of staff in all of the most senior positions. It's only natural. He assumes that if he puts them there, he'll have bought their loyalty, but you can't buy experience, and he's too keen to sweep all of that away," said Eufame.

"What does that have to do with me?"

"It's simple. I cannot directly oppose the prince. To do so would be considered treason, and I rather like my head attached to my neck. However, by undermining his coronation, I thereby undermine his rule, and make it a lot more difficult for him to impose his authority."

"So you *wanted* me to ruin his coronation for you?" Jyx bit back a sob. He couldn't believe he'd failed to see her plan.

"In a word, yes. You've succeeded admirably, although I'm still furious about the destruction of my belongings. I didn't exactly factor that into the equation. Don't be so upset, Jyx. One of the men the prince sought to replace is in charge of the Underground City, and the intended newcomer wanted to sweep away the slums."

"My mother!"

"Yes, Jyx, your mother. Now, I recognised that she would not exactly be safe there, even if Rattadamn stayed in office, since the prince would no doubt be out for blood. So I've had her moved. I won't say where, as walls have ears, even here, but she and your siblings are perfectly safe. I'm not entirely heartless."

Jyx managed a weak smile, though the thought that his mother might think he'd made such a mess of his academic career, indeed of his life, provoked a fresh wave of tears.

"In a way, your recklessness has saved an entire portion of the city. No one will ever know, except you, me, and the Wolfkin, but it's a valiant deed, nonetheless."

Eufame smiled, and for the first time since he met her, Jyx could see a faint glimmer of humanity within her icy shell. She wiped his eyes, and squeezed his hand.

"Now Jyx. This won't hurt...much."

Eufame pressed her cold lips to his forehead, a perverse goodbye kiss, and stepped away from the slab. She walked to the sigil nearest the door, and clapped her hands. The sigil glowed white beneath her feet, and a chant in an ancient tongue filled the chamber with whispers and screams. She walked to each sigil in turn, following the perimeter of the circle counter-clockwise, until each sigil pulsated with energy.

Jyx wished he could raise his arms, to press his hands against his ears and block out the fearful noises emanating from Eufame's throat. The chant changed key, and became an insistent, malevolent thrum. Jyx's ears hurt to hear it, to hear the minor key of death played out within the symphony of time. He caught sight of Eufame, oblivious to the effects of her chant. She raised her arms, and beams of light shot upward from the sigils. They collided at the tip of the obelisk.

"I will see you again, Jyximus Faire!" screamed Eufame.

The light shot down from the obelisk in a single beam. It passed through Jyx like a white-hot fire, and shock tore the scream from his throat. Bilious clouds of black filled his vision, and a cacophony of tolling bells assaulted his ears.

An instant later, Jyx ceased to be.

CHAPTER 12

Jyx opened his eyes—at least, that's what he thought he'd done. One moment he couldn't see, and the next he could, but he knew he had no body, much less any eyes to see.

I exist.

The swirling grey mist of the World Beyond floated around and through him. Dark shades slid beyond him. He felt vibrations somewhere within his own shade that felt like greetings, and he tried to nod in response.

Something large and black made its way through the mist. Jyx gained an impression of flapping wings, and a consolidation of Time itself, and he tumbled away from the creature. The World Beyond lacked direction, and Jyx couldn't tell if he fell downward or upward or even if he spiralled in some figurative shape. He tried to clutch at himself, to keep himself from tattering apart in the wake of the beast.

I feel like a cobweb in the wind.

Jyx fought to think of all of the spells that he

knew, searching his being for the incantations and hexes he'd spent so long memorising. They were all gone, washed clean from his mind when he left the mortal plane.

There is no need for magic here.

The thought made the remnants of Jyx run cold. He couldn't remember a time in his life when he didn't have at least the rudiments of magic at his fingertips.

But I don't have a life, not anymore. It's just me, and this, forever.

Jyx looked around, watching the other wraiths drift between each other. Some of them paused and acknowledged one another, soundless greetings passing through the silent space, but most seemed directionless. Many of them seemed to be empty, as though the spark of the soul had gone out entirely.

Is that what Eufame condemned me to?

Jyx would have cried if he'd had the body to do so. His mind strayed to the morning meeting with Dean Whittaker, and he wished with everything he had left that the dean had expelled him. A lifetime struggling in the Underground City was no real life, but at least it was better than this non-existence.

"Jyximus Faire..."

Jyx looked around at the sound of his name. It echoed around him, the syllables seeking his essence in the depths of the mist. More words, strangely familiar yet utterly alien, resounded in the air around him, and he felt himself compelled to follow their trail. The echo led towards a golden light, surrounded by dancing fireflies. Jyx didn't know where the portal led, but he knew he wanted to find out.

CHAPTER 13

Jyx's eyes shot open and he looked up at an inverted obelisk embedded in the ceiling. His lungs screamed for air and he opened his mouth, wheezing and gulping in equal measure. Steady hands slid beneath him and sat him up. He recognised the slab, and the empty cages on the walls. He recognised the mother-of-pearl sigils in the black marble floor, and the formidable ginger Wolfkin, impassive several feet away. He recognised Eufame.

"Welcome back, Jyx."

"Wha—"

"Welcome back to the House of the Long Dead." The pale necromancer general leaned over him. The memory of the last time he'd seen this room jolted in his mind.

"You killed me."

"Technically, I removed your soul from your body and ushered it along to the World Beyond. I didn't actually touch your mortal frame itself, which is what I'd need to do to kill you." Eufame peered into his face, her sharp nose just inches from his. She smelled of violets and alchemical powder and Jyx shuddered.

"Wha—"

"Oh do try to be a little more interesting, Jyx. I separated your soul from your body, and for a few moments they existed simultaneously in different realms, and all you can say is 'Wha'?"

"Moments?" Jyx felt he'd been gone for years.

"Exactly two minutes, by my count." Eufame made a show of consulting her wrist but Jyx didn't remember her wearing a watch. Time still felt sticky, and he tried to keep still until the nausea subsided.

"Was that my punishment?" he asked.

"Part of it."

"Part of it?"

"Jyx, it will take a little more than a simple body-soul separation to earn my forgiveness, and the prince won't exactly be satisfied, either. The sooner you realise that, the better."

Eufame turned away and walked towards one of the cages. She unhooked it from the wall and the Wolfkin helped her lift it down. It met the marble floor with a resounding clang. Jyx winced, his senses still tender from their excursion into the World Beyond.

"What's that for?" he asked.

"I did tell you that you'd been condemned to the Perpetual Death. I've had a communication from the prince while you were gone, and he was pleased with the idea. Of course, he has no actual idea what it entails, but at least he hasn't ordered an execution."

"Why do you need a cage?"

Eufame and the Wolfkin brought it closer. Jyx saw it was large enough to hold him if he sat cross-legged on its solid iron floor. A menacing smile crept across Eufame's face, and Jyx darted a glance at the door. He tried to wiggle his toes to test the strength in his legs, but he couldn't even muster a twitch. Running was out of the question.

"I'm sure even you're not stupid enough to think that I have nothing better to do than stand here to recall your soul every time I send you into the World Beyond."

"Every time you send me?"

"That's the point of the Perpetual Death. You die and you come back, again and again." Eufame drew a sigil above the lock, and the cage door sprang open. Jyx gulped.

"Can't you just tell the prince you're doing this? He's not going to check, is he?"

"I'm going to ignore that, Jyx. Don't forget, your little stunt might have ruined the procession as I planned, but it also damaged some of my irreplaceable possessions, and forced me to scrap some valuable alchemical work."

Eufame and the Wolfkin each seized one of Jyx's arms, and hauled him from the slab. Jyx wanted to lash out with his feet, to cause some kind of scene, but his limbs refused to obey his commands. He hung from their hands until they forced him into the cage. The Wolfkin arranged his legs into a crossed position, and slammed the door shut.

"You're going to experience the World Beyond a lot more, Jyx. I promise you that," said Eufame.

The Wolfkin hoisted the cage onto its back and carried it across the chamber to an empty alcove. The cage slid inside, surrounding Jyx on three sides with solid black marble.

"Forever?"

"Well...probably not. So it might be worthwhile for you make mental notes while you're there."

The Wolfkin left the chamber. Eufame stood in the centre beside the slab, and produced a small silver globe from inside her sleeve. She balanced it on its pointed tip on the slab, and set it spinning. Sparks scattered across the marble and sounds issued from the globe. Jyx winced as he recognised Eufame's awful profane chant. White light sparked from the tip of the obelisk as the recorded chant grew louder. Jyx pushed to the front of the cage and looked up; for the first time, he noticed strips of metal running from the tip of the obelisk up to the ceiling, and around the walls to the alcoves.

The necromancer general's globe let out a primal scream and the energy raced down the metal strip to Jyx's alcove. It made contact with the iron cage, and enveloped Jyx's hands, still wrapped around the bars. Jyx's scream joined that of Eufame's as, for the second time that day, he ceased to exist.

TO BE CONTINUED...

Did you enjoy *The Necromancer's Apprentice*? Don't forget to leave a review on your favourite retailer's website – even if it's only short. It helps readers find better books to read from online stores.

Thank you!

At the start of this book, I promised you an exclusive prequel story. So if you enjoyed this book, and you want to get to know Eufame Delsenza a little better, then join my mailing list to receive *The Skeleton in the Floor*!

Find out exactly *how* a skeleton ended up embedded in the floor of the House of the Long Dead. Meet Eufame's first apprentice, Faro Pixenby. Enjoy more intrigue, betrayal, and powerful magick!

Go to;
http://www.icysedgwick.com/skeleton/
to get your free copy.

Keep reading to get a preview of book two, *The Necromancer's Rogue*.

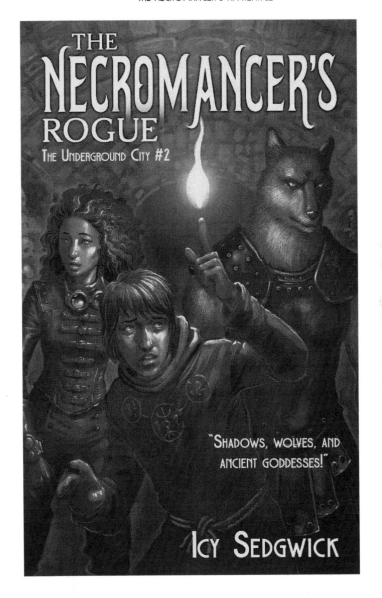

THE
NECROMANCER'S
ROGUE
THE UNDERGROUND CITY #2

"SHADOWS, WOLVES, AND
ANCIENT GODDESSES!"

ICY SEDGWICK

CHAPTER ONE

The Almighty Crack, as the sound would be known in the days and weeks after the dust finally settled, was first heard by those waiting to petition the priestesses at Beseda's Shrine. Being in the catacombs below the Underground City, they were closest to the epicentre, and reported the noise as being like that of the Great Cannon of the City Above. Several visitors chose to remain in the shrine to claim Beseda's protection from the unseen foe they believed was attacking the city. When no pillaging forces appeared, the priestesses ushered out the petitioners.

The inhabitants of the Underground City heard it next, and later described it as a muffled roar that roused the sick and drunk alike from their beds. Many of the slum-dwellers believed it to be the gates between the cities finally rolling shut, and prepared to raise their voices in protest. Calm was restored when they reached the mighty Lockevar's Gate and realised it was still open, and they drifted away to return to their subterranean lives, the mysterious noise forgotten for the time being.

Those in the Canal District of the City Above heard the crack and thought the foundations of their homes had burst at last. They believed they would be flooded, and scurried around the lower storeys of their homes until they noticed no intake of water, and went back to their daily business.

The Almighty Crack was quietly observed in the Magickal Quarter, where the Academy's diviner ominously proclaimed the beginning of a period of mourning. The rest of the staff ignored him and instead blamed an experiment gone wrong in one of the classrooms, and the diviner failed to realise it was the only time in his life that his prediction had been right. The staff couldn't find the source of the noise and promptly returned to lessons.

Yet in a forgotten tomb below the Underground City, beyond the catacombs of Beseda's Shrine, a statue adopted a new pose. Long ago the figure had stood tall and proud, a warrior goddess enjoying the glory of her city, but now she pressed her back against the wall, stone arms clasped around cold knees. Her mane of hair curled in limestone tendrils around her forehead, hiding her fearsome face from view. Her discarded spear lay on the floor, its shaft split down the middle. A plumed helmet rested on its side near the door. Few would have recognised the fragments of chipped stone at her side as being a heart.

None would have remembered the name of this being, once terrible and formidable, yet they would eventually come to share her pain as the Heart of the City finally broke.

CHAPTER TWO

Monte McThwaite sat at the table in the pub. A book lay in front of him, bound in leather so black it absorbed all of the feeble light that flickered in its direction. No name was emblazoned on the spine or cover.

"Seems like a pretty big book to be lugging around everywhere." He knocked back the last of his whiskey, winced, and put down the glass.

"Important things are no burden." The man across the table smiled, displaying ferocious rows of dagger-like teeth.

Monte shuddered.

"You won't find many down here wanting to read." Monte gestured to the pub's other patrons, a motley crew of drunks and fishwives back from the coast. A troll in the corner threw him a hard glare, and Monte looked away. His last encounter with a troll had left him without a sense of smell for an entire month.

"Good. The contents of this book are not for them." The man returned the troll's glare, apparently less worried about its strength than Monte.

"So why are you telling me about it then?"

"Firstly, you are familiar with death, and have a certain tolerance of it. This is helpful to my cause. Secondly, I get the sense you can actually read."

Monte tried not to beam with pride. He'd always wanted to be seen as an educated man and not the gravedigger he actually was. This stranger, this man, had noticed what everyone else ignored.

"I can read, but I'm not the only one in here – you see that guy by the bar?" Monte pointed out a tall, gaunt man with long grey hair and a matted beard. His hangdog expression told Monte that the four pints of Bezziwig's Broken Heart Basher had not yet begun to work.

"I do."

"That's old Crompton Daye. He's a wizard."

"Ah, a wizard will not suit my purposes. I need someone who can read but is not keen to use their mind unsupervised. Someone who will not think for themselves."

Monte scowled, his previous pride deflated.

"Oh don't look so piqued, my good man. I simply mean that wizards are too unpredictable and contrary. Their moods change on a whim. No, I need someone solid, and dependable. Reliable. The salt of the earth."

"What do you need this someone for?" Monte

tried to recall how the conversation had started, but he could only remember arriving at the pub at the end of his shift, and then the book, that awful big black book. A gaping hole opened in his memory between the two events. Had the man approached him, or was it the other way around?

"I'm currently conducting what you might call an experiment, although it's also a bit of a quest, in its own way. Whatever you call it, it is vitally important, and could very well change the course of these delightful twin cities."

Monte raised his eyebrow in reply.

"You see, my strong friend, that is a book of last words, and I need someone to help me once I've heard the last words I'm listening for."

"Eh?"

The man leaned closer and lowered his voice. "I visit the dying as they lie on their death beds, and I collect their last words before they fade from the air and disappear into nothingness. My work is partly out of a desire to record for posterity the final statements of the dead. You could consider it a work of social history."

"But which ones are you looking for?"

"Excuse me?"

"You said you needed my help once you'd heard the ones you were looking for." Monte looked down at the book, wondering how many of those pages had been filled – and with what.

"Ah, my good man, you are sharper than you appear."

Monte beamed again. His smile widened when

another drink appeared on the table before him. He looked around to thank the waitress but saw no one.

"Well, I need your assistance because I believe that among the citizens of this great city is one who knows the location of a certain artefact. It goes by many names, but the one I prefer is the Heart of the City. He who possesses the heart –"

"Possesses the City. Well, Cities," finished Monte.

"Exactly. You know the story, then?"

"Every child in the Underground City does, though I can't speak for Above."

"Indulge me." The man smiled again.

Monte forced himself not to look at his teeth. Why did a man need so many teeth?

"When the Underground City was first hacked out of the earth, a warrior goddess protected them from the things they awoke in the depths. She loved the city fiercely when it was finished, and she died in battle, fighting a fearsome hydra. She killed it but she left her Heart to the city so that it may always be protected. My old mum always said if we need her again, we just need to find her Heart and she'll come back. But no one knows where it is anymore. I thought it was a bedtime story for children."

"Many men do, Monte. That is precisely why no one knows where the Heart currently rests – no one believes it exists. But I do." The man tapped himself on the chest with one long, skinny finger.

"So what has this got to do with your book?"

"I began my project in order to gain access to

people on their death beds, which is ultimately the only place where man will speak the truth, and I'm yet to hear what I'm waiting for. Though I believe I shall, and soon, and I shall require your help once I do in order to locate the Heart itself."

"Say it does exist. What do you want it for?" asked Monte. Rumours tore around the Underground City about people disappearing from the street, the City Above Militia conducting beatings whenever they felt like it in the slums, and even wholesale demolitions near Lockevar's Gate, but surely things weren't so bad that anyone was looking for the Heart of the City.

"I told you, I'm a historian. An artefact like that should be on display. It shouldn't be hidden away in some cold hole somewhere. So, can I rely on your dogged determination and admirable assistance?"

"I've already got a job, though," replied Monte. He'd heard stories about the type of work men could find in the pub – and the trouble that usually followed. Besides, Myrtle would kill him if she found out he'd given up the grave digging for nothing. The work didn't pay well, but any salary was worth having in the Underground City.

"I realise that, which is why I shall pay you more. How about a gold crown now, and a half crown for every week that you are in my employ?"

A flash of gold streaked across the man's knuckles. Monte's gaze followed its every movement.

"I'll do it." Monte agreed before he'd even made up his mind to do so. The man reached underneath the table to pass Monte the coin and he shoved it into his trouser pocket. Myrtle would be so pleased that she might even be nice to him.

"Excellent. My name is Mr Gondavere." The man held out his hand across the table. Monte shook it, feeling its cold, papery texture beneath his own flesh.

"When do we start, sir?" he asked.

"How about now? I do believe there's a man upstairs who won't be in this world much longer."

Mr Gondavere rose and headed towards the bar before Monte could ask him how he knew that. Mr Gondavere stopped to exchange words with the barkeeper, who widened his eyes and nodded. Mr Gondavere gestured with a nod for Monte to follow, and Monte passed through the hatch in the bar and up the back stairs, wondering exactly what he'd gotten himself into.

The Necromancer's Rogue is out now!

MEET THE AUTHOR

Icy Sedgwick was born in the north east of England, and is currently based in Newcastle. She had her first book, the pulp Western adventure, *The Guns of Retribution*, published in September 2011. When she isn't writing or teaching, she's working on a PhD in Film Studies, knitting, exploring graveyards, or watching history documentaries.

CONNECT WITH ICY!

Website:
http://www.icysedgwick.com/

Twitter:
https://twitter.com/IcySedgwick/

Instagram:
https://www.instagram.com/icysedgwick/

Facebook:
https://www.facebook.com/miss.icy.sedgwick/

Pinterest:
https://www.pinterest.co.uk/icysedgwick/

G+:
https://plus.google.com/+IcySedgwick/about

THE POST CREDITS SCENE

If it's good enough for Marvel, it's good enough for me!

Anyway, you've made it all the way back here. I've already invited you to join my list, where you'll get a free copy of *The Skeleton in the Floor* just for signing up.

You'll also get one monthly email (I'm not a spam factory, after all) containing a free short story, book recommendations, and other cool stuff I think you might like.

Don't worry that I'll just bombard you with "BUY MY BOOK!" That isn't my style. I want you to get something out of hanging out with me!

But if you sign up, you'll also get the chance to join my review team, which means you get free copies of my books before they're released, and all you have to do is pop a short review on Amazon!

If that sounds like something you'd like to do, sign up at

http://www.icysedgwick.com/skeleton/

I'll see you there!

Printed in Great Britain
by Amazon